HOMEWARD BOUND

Jon Foyt

Andrew Benzie Books
Walnut Creek, California

Published by Andrew Benzie Books
www.andrewbenziebooks.com

Printed in the United States of America

First Edition: March 2018

10 9 8 7 6 5 4 3 2 1

ISBN 978-1-941713-68-6

Cover and book design by Andrew Benzie

*This novel is dedicated to Helen,
who has imbued me with a sense of compassion
and a renewed love of life as I search for its deepest meanings.*

TABLE OF CONTENTS

ACKNOWLEDGMENTS

The author wishes to acknowledge the assistance, in regard to the Los Patricios, from Dr. Donald Sharpes of Arizona State University, Patrick Goggins and Claudia O'Callaghan of the Irish Literary and Historical Society of San Francisco.

PROLOGUE

Sean O'Flannery, a stormy ocean crossing away from Galway and seeking refuge from the potato famine devastating Ireland, was looking forward to relief from hunger while pursuing the economic opportunities he'd heard about and that were promised in the United States. Hopefully, or so he and his fellow Irishmen had been led to believe, here would be waiting a new and fresh life with plenty of food, a woman for each, followed by a family, yes, and an ongoing life of happiness, being joined by fellow Irishmen and women fleeing the famine raging across the Emerald Isle. To a man, they envisioned a bright new life here in this, their adopted country.

CHAPTER ONE:
LOS PATRICIOS

The camaraderie Sean felt being with his fellow émigrés in the promised land, so they each had come to think, was strong enough to last a lifetime. But now they were all facing discrimination whenever they crossed over from their familiar Irish culture and entered the established and dominating American value system. It was proving to be an unwelcome bridge each of them tried to cross every day as they went about looking for jobs—"Not Hiring Irish." As Sean reflected to his cohorts, it was that way trying to do just about anything in this new land. As the days passed, Sean and his countrymen reluctantly grew disillusioned with their chosen land and its fading promises.

"Talk about a famine," Sean complained to Father Andrew, his priest in a church in the Manhattan Irish section. "Father, life here in the United States is a famine of opportunity with the added element of prejudice against me and all us Irish blokes."

Father Andrew O'Malley smiled knowingly, empathizing with Sean's disappointment. But the priest offered no guidance for solving the dilemma. After more conversations, the holy man suggested to Sean that the solution for him and his comrades was to join the U. S. Army. "At least you can get a wee income, a uniform for clothing, and a place to eat and sleep every night. I have encouraged a number of our lads to do just that," To Sean's expression of interest, Father Andrew advised, "A recruiting sergeant, who is a member of our parish is coming tomorrow evening. You and your fellow immigrants should talk to him."

"But, Father, can you explain our disillusionment? What is behind this prejudice against us Irish? Where does it come from? The English? The Protestants? I mean, this isn't Ulster in the North."

Father Andrew stroked his graying beard and slowly replied, hoping to clarify for his new parishioner the facts of immigrant life in

1

the United States. "Jobs, My Son. Jobs. Those who were here first—whether they're English or German or Scots, or wherever, look upon each of you fresh Irish immigrants as hungry, maybe starving, and thus willing to work for less money, clearly a lot less. You got off the boat starved and, they fear, will work for virtually no wages at all. As a result of you lads being in the work force and competing with them and willing to work for virtually nothing, they fear losing their jobs, along with their wives as, suddenly being unemployed, their wellbeing will vanish. From those fears spring their ugly expressed hate and their biases. It's not your fault. I try in my sermons to cite scripture in my attempt to dispel such prejudices, but it's not an easy assignment for me or for any member of the cloth."

"What, Father, can we do as a group of hungry Irish lads, to change their minds?"

The priest laughed and then apologized for his mirth. "I'm sorry, Sean, you ask a question for which I have no answer, nor does anyone in the Church or in our Irish society, I'm afraid." The holy man paused, adding, "Take my advice, Sean, and talk to the recruiting sergeant tomorrow. Think seriously about joining the American Army."

After another frustrating and unproductive day, no longer back in his familiar Irish environs in Galway, and now experiencing being on the bottom of the social ladder, the unemployed Sean came to the church the next evening. Along with his fellow immigrants from all over Ireland, they talked to the uniformed Sergeant Lou Parnell, a cousin, so he bragged, of the famed Irish revolutionary. That evening, Sean and his lads joined up and became inductees in the Army of the United States of America.

As raw recruits, they found they had an unfair rank even below that of a buck private. They were thus regarded in the minds of the American enlisted men and even the officers in the expanding Army, the boys from Ireland being cast into the lowest levels of the military. Being at the bottom of the order, they were always assigned the least desirous of military tasks and routines. Grunt work, Sean soon called it, to the agreement of his fellow Irish lads. And then when they wanted to go to Catholic Mass, they were told that the Army doesn't allow Catholic services. In fact, two of the lads were put in the stockade for two days, just for asking. The others were told they should read their Bibles, or else attend Protestant services.

Meanwhile, Sean learned, the United States Army was expanding its numbers and it weaponry. Southerners wanted a strong army to fight feared slave revolts, as well as possible invasions of freed slaves from the Caribbean. Concurrently, in lock step with the westward viewing nation, President James K. Polk was advocating an expansionist policy of what the media authority John O'Sullivan of *Harper's Weekly* later labeled as Manifest Destiny. As more and more voters nationwide began to champion Polk's intentions, his slogan grew into a national cry endorsing westward continental aggression aimed toward reaching the shores of the shimmering Pacific Ocean. Nothing and nobody—indigenous Native Americans, Texans, earlier arrival Mexicans, colonizing British, fur-trading French, or the devil himself, so journalists wrote and politicians extolled—was going to stop the American republic from accomplishing its territorial aims in realizing its purported God-given destiny.

At the same time, tensions in Texas were rising over a territory dispute with neighboring Mexico. Both countries, and especially the new and aggressive citizens of the independent Texas, the Tejanos, claimed the luscious farmland lying from the Nueces River south to the Rio Grande. The Tejanos in San Antonio were threatening to take over this disputed land, and the Mexican Federals were threatening to shoot anyone crossing into what they lovingly now regarded as Mexican territory—for it had recently become their own land, following the national freedom they had fought for and gained from oppressive Spain, culminating in celebration of their independence as a country on Cinco de Mayo in 1820.

Soon Sean and his recruited Irish lads, now trained in weapons of war and under military discipline, having been fed a little and paid a bit, were shipped off to South Texas wearing their new uniforms of the U. S. Army.

*   *   *

Not long after the Irishmen arrived on the Texas frontier with Mexico, gunshots erupted as a contingent of Mexican soldiers crossed the Rio Grande and assaulted U.S. soldiers near the Texas town of Brownsville. Within days, Sean and his fellow Irish soldiers found themselves on the front line, the very front line, the most vulnerable front line, while their American military counterparts huddled on safer ground to the rear. When food came and ammunition supplies arrived, little of either made its way up to the front lines. Sean realized discrimination hadn't abetted, battle or no, war or no, patriotism or no. Nothing had changed, as Sean remarked to his fellow immigrants. The angst in their war of discontent took on new dimensions as the Irish lads lamented their lower lot.

One day during the smoke and noise of battle, a uniformed Mexican messenger, waving a white flag of truce in one hand and some sort of document in the other, approached their position. Sean motioned the Mexican soldier forward as they held their fire. The document the Mexican was carrying and handed to Sean was a letter addressed to the Irishmen fighting in the U. S. Army. As the messenger advised in good English, it was not really a letter but instead, an official proclamation addressed to them and bearing the signature and official military seal of Generalissimo Antonio Lopez de Santa Anna.

One of the Irish lads was literate, having attended a school in Dublin. He asked the messenger for the document. It was in English. He told his comrades it was really an invitation. He read the message to the soldiers gathering around.

To all you brave Irish heroes, hail and greeting: The democracy of Mexico welcomes you and invites you to join our ranks and seek revenge against the Yankee oppressors. We'll double your wages, and some of you can become officers in the Mexican Army. We'll call you Los Patricios after your beloved and respected Saint Patrick! Come on over to freedom and join your fellow Catholics across the Rio Grande in Meico—Now! Your friend and patron, Generalissimo Santa Anna.

One after the other, the lads expressed their surprise and indeed their excitement. "It's like the English offering us jobs in Buckingham Palace working for the Queen," Sean didn't hesitate long before telling them. "I say we do it." The others talked about the Mexican offer at length. "If we do it, there's no going back," one declared, that is, "back to the U. S." Another said, "They'll hang us if they capture us." "We won't let that happen," another assured the group as they formed into a circle of comrades. Without prolonged debate, for their minds were working in unison, they began to form a consensus. One by one, they voted. The outcome was unanimous. Yes, they vowed, they would desert, cross the Rio Grande, their Rubicon, and join up with the Mexican Army.

So, Sean O'Flannery and his compatriots waited for the dark and waded across the Rio Grande into Mexico where they were greeted in friendship and camaraderie by a Mexican general and his fellow soldiers. They were soon fitted for Mexican army uniforms and assigned weapons. A banner proclaiming them as *Los Patricios* was given to them as a morale builder. They proudly hoisted the flag as a symbol of their new *Los Patricios* regiment. As they basked in welcoming cheers from other Mexican solders, a frocked priest blessed them in Spanish and then in English. Then they ate quantities of chorizo sausage and enchiladas. And proudly they waved their banner to the cheers of their fellow Mexican troops.

"This is more like it, what we came for on that long ocean voyage," Sean remarked to the cheers of his fellow immigrant Irishmen.

*   *   *

The Mexican-American War raged on. Under command of General Winfield Scott, American troops crossed the Rio Grande en masse and began a steady advance southward toward Mexico City. The Mexicans, in battle after battle, gave up ground grudgingly and stubbornly. *Los Patricios*, led by Sean, distinguished themselves in the fighting while enjoying equality and camaraderie with their fellow Mexican soldiers.

Later, during the bloody Battle of Chapultepec Castle, some *Patricios* were captured and promptly executed by the victorious Americans. In the melee after the battle, and during his subsequent retreat, Santa Anna summoned Sean to his field tent and told him, "You have fought bravely, Sean, leading your Irish compatriots. As your reward, as a Mexican generalissimo, I am herewith awarding you a Land Grant. It is up north in Alta California near Yerba Buena."

"Where's that, Sir?"

"In lush farmland. Should you survive this war, you must make your way there by ship. General Vallejo can show you the boundaries of the grant. But I fear that soon we are going to be forced by treaty to give up much of our lands to the Americans. Our struggle is going to be done with before long. In fact, I am meeting with the American generals at Guadalupe-Hidalgo within a few weeks."

And Santa Anna was gone with his tent and the remains of his

Mexican army, which was soon forced to surrender. In 1848, Santa Anna signed the Treaty of Guadalupe-Hidalgo, in which Mexico ceded territories stretching north into Colorado, most of New Mexico except for Las Cruces, all of Texas, most of Arizona except for Tucson, the entirety of Nevada, and all of Alta California in exchange for his treaty signature and a few million U.S. dollars.

CHAPTER TWO:
A GAME OF CHANCE

S ean had never imagined himself being in a financial and social position where he would actually be the owner of land. Land in any size. Land on which he might live and farm. In Galway almost all the land was owned, likely in perpetuity, by English lords, who rented out parcels of land to farmers who, themselves in need of revenue, rented even smaller parcels to other starving farmers, who then often split their little rental into even tinier plots to rent to another struggling farmer. Usually the size of the sub-rented land was only a few square meters. It was customary to delineate each of these plots, no matter how small, by a crude stonewall. The Irish landscape, as a result, had become a jigsaw puzzle of meandering hand-built rock walls running every which way. The smallest of these parcels was too tiny to make economic sense in the growing of any crop or by raising enough animals to sustain the sub-renter's existence. Poverty prevailed. And then had come the potato famine.

As a result of these rented and sub-rented land divisions, actual land ownership for an Irishman was a distant, if not abstract idea, clearly a concept unfamiliar to Sean and his fellow Irish soldiers.

Now, as a reward for his heroism in fighting the Americans, he was being offered something called a land grant. What did that mean? This was a term as foreign as were the lands in which the *Los Patricios* had fought and on which many of them had died.

Generalisimo Santa Anna had told him that the land in this grant was located in a place called Alta California. Sean had asked the general, "What does a land grant mean?"

Holding up the brown parchment delineating the grant, Santa Anna pointed to the parcel's boundaries running irregularly along the edges and shown in black ink. At the top were inverted V's, which the general said were mountains. At the lower edge wavy lines, as he said, representing the waters of a large bay. "This is now your land,

Sean," Santa Anna told him. "Build a house, raise crops. It's your own hacienda, my hero. It is your sovereignty. You must go there, to the Customs House in Monterey and register your domain." He handed Sean another document and said, "This is a personal letter addressed to General Mariano Guadalupe Vallejo, introducing you as a hero of Mexico. General Vallejo is an important man in Alta California. See him if you have any questions about the land grant and for directions to your lands." Sean expressed his thanks, bowed and then, standing at attention, saluted the departing Mexican general.

*   *   *

Curious to see his lands, Sean vowed to himself he would go north as soon as possible. First, he bid an emotional goodbye to his fellow soldiers in the *Las Patricios* brigade, most of whom had decided to remain in Mexico. He told them if they needed land to farm, he'd accommodate their requests if they would come to Alta California and see him.

After one last night of revelry and soldierly comradeship, Sean set off for the north by making his way to the port of Chiapas in time to part with his last stash of American money, retrieved from off fallen U.S. soldiers, and book passage on the next sailing ship bound for Monterey in Alta California.

The ocean-going journey on the old passenger sailboat struggling north from the Mexican port was rough, its progress slow. Nevertheless, Sean clutched his bundle of Mexican money from his pay as a *Los Patricio*, intent on adding to it with American dollars to be won, he was confident, at the ship's gambling tables.

By the third night out, the waters had calmed and the gaming tables were open. Strolling on deck, Sean struck up a conversation with the ship's Captain, who pointed out that the distant shoreline was Baja California. He said, later that evening they would be crossing the border between the two Mexican provinces of Baja and Alta and enter the waters of California. Sean said that's where he was going to inspect his land grant awarded him by General Santa Anna. Proudly he mentioned to the captain his role with the *Los Patricios* in the recent war. The captain acknowledged his service, wished him a pleasant journey, and went to the ship's wheelhouse.

By well into evening, the ship was smoothly making its way north with the help of a gentle southern breeze. His courage up, Sean chose a gaming table where a bedraggled foreign-looking older man and a soldier, probably just discharged from the Mexican Army, were sitting. He thought he ought to do well against these two seemingly unsophisticated players, and he motioned to the vacant chair as if asking if he might join them. The bedraggled man spoke to Sean, "Wellkommen." German, Sean concluded, acknowledging the man's greeting with a nod. Sean sat down, stacking in front of him the array of chips he had purchased with his Mexican dollars from the purser. He was ready to play.

The German watched Sean's movements and visually seemed to tabulate the total value of his chips. He then acknowledged Sean's presence with a guttural sound that seemed to signal they were about to begin. The same Mexican soldier tried a smile that the German shut off with a stern look as he dealt a hand of what he announced to be the nine-card game of Brag. Sean had once played the game in Ireland, and knew it derived from the British. So much in Ireland derived from the British, Sean lamented to himself. What did life here derive from, Sean wondered. Mexico, for sure, even though they had lost the war. Or was it from the Americans? A comely lady came by their table. She smiled at Sean and offered him a Tequila from off the tray she was carrying. As he sipped the elixir and admired the woman, Sean concluded that Mexican customs must still dominate on board this sailing ship.

So, Sean, along with the German and then the Mexican, anted their chips. Nine cards were dealt face down to each of the three men. Looking at his hand, Sean tried to make his sets, without much luck. As time passed in the warm breeze, Sean realized the cards weren't acting right, but he kept playing, hoping for the better luck he was certain was due him on the next hand and the next after that. The night went on and the ship sailed farther north. The moonlight allowed a distant sighting of the rugged and remote Pacific Coastline of Alta California. That is, if anyone was looking beyond the gaming table toward the eastern horizon.

Sean saw more hints of smiles from the German as his sets carried most of the hands that followed, regardless of who at the table dealt the cards. Virtually each time, the German, who let Sean and the Mexican know between hands that his name was Baron Wilhelm von

Herzog, scraped his winnings onto his growing pile of chips. Even after more rounds of bets, Sean's confidence continued as he told himself that his sets would soon prevail. But as more time went by and more losses went down, and he tipped more of the Tequila, Sean began to realize that things weren't going well for him. His stack of chips was dwindling. More hands followed, the Mexican dealing, then Sean, then back to the German.

Meanwhile, the pretty woman had brought more Tequila and told him her name was Elsa. This time Elsa sat on Sean's lap, twirling his Irish curls in her long fingers. By now Sean had become obsessed with the color of her nails and how they matched one or more of the many colors in her skimpy skirt, protruding from which he admired her shapely legs. Still the card sets were not unfolding well for Sean. Distracted by her, he found it difficult to focus on the cards in his hand. And as more hands were played, he willingly accepted yet another Tequila from the attentive beauty, who he now realized had not sat on the lap of the other two card players.

On into the evening, the German stretched, yawned, and announced he was tired and was going to quit their little game, but first, from behind his rising pile of chips, he said it was time to settle up their bets for the evening. "In American dollars," he advised in his uncompromising Teutonic voice.

As the German spoke, the ship's captain came by their table, seemingly on another inspection of the ship. He saluted the German who nodded. "Settling up for the night... are we?" the Captain said as he addressed the three gamblers. He added in the firm tone of voice of a ship's captain in charge of his vessel, "In American dollars, of course. That's the rule on my ship."

Sean looked up and respectfully advised the captain, "Sir, I have only Mexican money from my stint as a Mexican soldier in the recent war."

Without waiting for the captain's reply, Baron Herzog decreed, "Your money's no good here," He looked up at the captain for verification. The ship's captain nodded emphatically. To Sean, the German said, "You, Sir, owe me real money."

The captain bid them good night, advising, "I'll be on duty." As he turned to leave, Sean saw the handle of the American military pistol tucked snugly in the holster hanging from his thick belt. The weapon was obviously ready for the draw. But the captain didn't leave. Instead, he stood there overseeing, as Baron Herzog demanded of Sean, "What else of value do you have?"

Growing uneasy, Sean reached for another shot of tequila, which Elsa promptly placed in his hand from off her tray. The smooth drink soothed his concerns only a bit, but didn't mitigate his anxiety, as he offered, "I have my Mexican Army pistol... back in my bunk... down below. It's German manufacture," he added, hoping its origin would satisfy the Baron.

The German stared at Sean intently, shaking his head and reiterating his question, this time in a firmer tone, "What else do you have?" As if to encourage Sean to respond, Elsa twirled his Irish curls once more.

Sean realized he was up against it with this demanding German, backed by the ship's captain, the on-board law and order. He almost stuttered as he said in his Irish brogue, "Well, I do have a Mexican land grant for some place up north, maybe it's about the size of a wee Irish plot of land. I don't know for sure. It's near some place called Yerba Buena."

"That's the name of a herb," Elsa announced.

Sean said, "Also a place, I think."

"Is it signed by General Santa Anna?" the German wanted to know.

Sean nodded.

"Let me see it."

Sean produced the rolled-up parchment.

The German and Elsa, in turn, examined the document. "It is indeed signed by the General," she announced. Smiling, she added, "I know his signature well." She looked at it again. "It is dated, Baron, before the Treaty was signed."

The German pressed Elsa, "But is it a valid document?"

"Yes, Baron, it appears to me to be authentic."

The German nodded at Elsa and pointed to the bottom of the document. Elsa took the cue, left and soon returned with a quill pen and a small ink well. The Baron said to Sean, "What's you full name?" Sean told him. Then the baron instructed, "Sign here," But first, above your signature write these words: I, Sean O'Flannery, willingly deed this land grant to Baron Wilhelm von Herzog."

Embarrassed, Sean admitted he couldn't write his name.

"Put an 'X' then." The Baron pointed where to do so and

addressed Elsa, "You write the words for him and then witness his mark."

After all, Sean thought, where was this place called Yerba Buena anyway? Maybe, after all, like Elsa had said, it was just a little tract of land that grew some plant of some sort. And, if it was a little parcel of land, what was he to do with land in this country so far away from Galway? Signing the parchment would get him off the hook for his evening's gambling losses, and he would still have his Mexican money. So, Sean took the quill pen, dipped it into the ink well and marked his 'X' after Elsa had written the words the Baron had instructed. Then she signed her full name as witness, dating it the day following Santa Anna's signature.

Sean disembarked at the port of Monterey. As he set foot on land, they were lowering the Mexican flag and hoisting the American flag. Sean noticed how the flags were similar in color, but different in design. He walked along the wharf. He asked about passage aboard a ship bound for Ireland. Everyone laughed. Why would anyone want to go back to Ireland? Sean didn't know why, but that's what he did. Eventually.

He had in mind putting up a statue on the main walkway of shops in the center of Galway honoring the magnificent Mexican General Santa Anna, along with his fellow *Los Patricios* fighting heroes, name after Irish name.

CHAPTER THREE:
A COLLEGE IN YERBA BUENA, A PRESENT
DAY GRADUATE ANTHROPOLOGY SEMINAR

Professor Dafnee Wiggins surveyed her seminar students sitting around the large table. Poised for intellectual action, their laptop computers open, their cell phones in hand. Six of them, three each in the gender mix. They were on track for their master's degree, if they could pass her strict seminar. Around campus, Dafnee's course was known as a challenge, and rightly so, she believed. She would not hesitate to tell anyone who wanted to enroll in her class that anthropology was more than a cursory study of cultures or an archaeological dig in the dirt looking for a tomb in Egypt or a lost city in some jungle in Central America.

She would tell them, "Anthropology is a search for the truth as to why a culture survives or doesn't survive. Ours is a search for answers, maybe not provable but answers supported by researched facts, logic, technology tools such as ground penetrating radar, and the product of your young minds at work. That sifts down to original thinking. Anthropology is a lifetime quest from which you must never retire."

Only those students who professed anthropology as the direction of their academic future had been permitted to sign onto her seminar. Oh, yes, maybe their acquiescence to her credo was perfunctory, but maybe, and she hoped, sincere on their part. As sincere as was her vow to her dying father that day he had succumbed to the sudden ice-cold wind chill engulfing their excavation on the shore of the Bering Strait in Alaska. She expressed an obligation to him and to research, which in the chill of that day, he had acknowledged in his final moments. From then on, Dafnee's vow to her father defined her role in academia and anthropology.

To her students, she began, "Here's your question to begin today's seminar: Why cannot a civilized society (as we know the word) provide sufficient and adequate housing for its people? Are we here in Yerba Buena the first culture to fail in this regard, or is such failure inevitable in today's world regardless of geographic location?"

Dafnee intended to go around her seminar room, allowing each student to express his or her hypothesis so she could evaluate and grade how they developed their thinking. She would make her critical notes as to how each student pursued their mental process and formulated their response. If she was to award a grade, it was not to be an alphabet but rather a comment grade as to their originality of thinking, how they presented their supporting arguments, their knowledge of their subject, and her impression of their competence and mannerisms as might befit their academic career in anthropology, along with the accompanying discipline required to fit into the scholarly scheme.

"It's not too hard to figure," said Gerald, the first student, as Dafnee sought answers in her clock-wise process. He said, "Think of the Roman Empire. How many people did they need to provide for in the vast territories they ruled? We don't read about the homeless in Rome. Maybe there were such unfortunates, but do they show up in the literature? Perhaps the homeless were not of significant cultural import back then, as they are today among us here in Yerba Buena."

The second student said, "There have always been migrations of peoples. During those mass migrations, people had to make do with makeshift homes. But then, Dr. Wiggins, you're asking about civilized societies. By definition civilized implies fixed, set in place, established locations. On the other hand, migrations were undertaken by itinerant or nomadic tribes, not established civilized societies. Ergo, they were all homeless."

Maria, the next student said, "But look at certain governments of so-called civilized cultures in the world today. They have fomented civil war, bombed their own residents so that thousands, maybe tens of thousands of their people became homeless, living in refugee camps in their own country or in neighboring nations. Either that, or they are trying to climb onto rubber rafts and float across the open sea to reach another land, where they will also be homeless until some group or another steps in and provides for them." Roxanne challenged. "But it is the people themselves who start revolutions, not governments. The people in that country initiated demonstrations expressing their grievances and advocating their rights in what has turned into outright civil war. Historically, governments have been complacent. The leaders will just sit there until enough people threaten them, threaten the status quo, threaten them, that is, the privileged people who are running the government. And then the government takes action, often oppressive and brutal."

"Revolution," said Ricki. "That's what it takes for governments to pay attention to what the people need, want, and sooner or later demand. And, she added, usually get, after many deaths and much hardship.

Dafnee acknowledged their contributions to the question and the several more that followed, which expressed thoughts along the lines of the first students.

Dafnee visually nodded toward the next student, announcing, "Raj, what do you have to say?" Raj was an immigrant from India and spoke with a bit of what the other students might dub "an accent." But, then today on campus, probably more people, students, faculty, and support staff spoke with "an accent" than didn't. After all, one came to ask the rhetorical question, why can't we each speak the same language with the same pronunciations? And then they would smile and nod their acceptance of the way things were.

Raj began, "My bachelor's degree is in geology. While listening to the others, and in reply to your question, Dr. Wiggins, I have developed this idea that ties to the geology of our earth."

Dafnee smiled, urging, "Tell us what you have come up with."

Raj pointed downward. "There's as much turmoil down below the surface of the Earth as there is up here among us on the surface."

"Meaning?" Dafnee asked.

"The Teutonic plates are moving, as are people up here. Down below, the movement causes earthquakes and volcanic eruptions. Up here, the movement of people causes dislocation. As a result, when people have been more or less isolated amongst themselves, over time their language changes, their culture changes as they adapt to changes in the world. In the same way, down below the movement of plates causes disruption and change. In other words, nothing stays the same. Not the rocks, not the people. The hills and mountains around us here are examples. They are here because of the uplifting from below, the earth's forces at work. On top, up here, the same differently described forces, but no less powerful, are at work. Thus, nothing stays the same. Change is constant." His going on suggested that he was hoping for approval, as he said, "New words, new phrases, new slang is being developed every day here on our campus."

Gerald reflected, "Change, Raj. Both below and on the surface."

"Yes, the uplift that created the four or five hills, or mountains that we have in this area. It was change from below—the uplift that did it. Not volcanic activity. That was elsewhere in the state, some significant distance from here."

Gerald went on, "But I'm concerned about the changes above ground. I mean, it's only been, what, 150 years since the Europeans came here to settle and rousted the Native Americans from off their lands. That's a short time in the geological calendar."

"A very short time," Raj agreed.

Gerald wanted to know, his voice almost belligerent, as he turned to address Dafnee and his fellow students, "What about that last large area of land in Yerba Buena that is both unpopulated and undeveloped? Will it ever change? What will it take to put all that land to a use that will provide enough housing that will satisfy the people?"

"You mean the homeless among us, right?" Raj asked.

"Right." Gerald gestured to his sleeping bag roll. Up here on the surface is where we need this Teutonic plate change you're talking about." He paused, choked up a bit and added, "For those of us who are homeless, the thousands of us, not only me and my friends here on campus."

Raj said, "That's my point." Before he could go on, the bell rang signaling class was over.

Dafnee nodded. "Next session, Raj, I want you and Gerald to develop your idea further."

As the students were leaving, Dafnee took Gerald aside and, concern in her voice, asked, "Are you getting places to sleep these nights?"

He frowned at the question. In an embarrassed tone, he allowed, "The Student Union has a few beds. They open at 5, and if I go there now I can be among the first in line."

Dafnee asked, "How many of them are you?"

Gerald thought. "Hundreds, I suppose. The student paper is trying to do a count, but a lot of students won't answer the questions because they think if they reveal they're homeless, it'll ruin their chances of getting a job when and if they can hang on long enough to graduate."

Trying to make her voice sound tender, Dafnee probed, "How long, Gerald, have you been among the homeless here on campus?"

"Since a fraternity wouldn't take me," he said, trying to make his voice sound indifferent. He smiled and, as if trying to explain, said, "A scholarship is fine. It pays tuition, books, but doesn't provide a student a place to sleep, certainly not at the astronomical prices for housing here."

CHAPTER FOUR:
MARCHERS AND DEMONSTRATORS
IN THE STREETS

"A hundred thousand... easily," Television Anchor Gloria Suchness declared. On the screen behind her appeared overhead views—first from atop a higher building, then from a low flying helicopter—followed by close ups of throngs of marchers carrying placards, hoisting signs. Many carried the multi-colored flag of human diversity. Some were pushing baby strollers. Some were thrusting fists toward the sky. As the cameras zoomed in, viewers could read the messages the marchers were brandishing: Give Us Homes; We Deserve Shelter; Homes for Pregnant Women; Families Want Homes; Where are the tiny houses you promised us? We are not vagrants; we have jobs; we vote! Remember Mark Hawthorne. Kill Rule 947. Support Disabled People Outside; Give Back Our Tents and Sleeping Bags the Police Took from us.

As one of the TV cameras picked up a leader of the march, Gloria declared, "There's Mary Montague, head of the Yerba Buena Homeless Agency. She's shouting into her usual purple and red striped bullhorn." Viewers watched those marchers close to her raise and lower their arms, fists clenched. "Mary shouted, "Protest and Resist! Love For Everyone." The crowd repeated the slogans in loud voices as the marchers, en mass, continued their blitzkrieg of protests.

"No violence yet," Gloria commented. But just then viewers watched a series of rocks crash through the large plate glass windows of a bank. Almost immediately sirens could be heard in the background. The intensity increased. A police riot squad was soon seen being deployed. Gloria said something—viewers could see her mouth moving and the concern on her face, but the din from the marchers' chants rose, drowning out her voice.

A reporter imbedded with the marchers was trying her best to select one of the marchers to interview. "I'm Matilda Monterey with Yerba Buena TV News, what's your name?"

"Suzanna. And my baby in my arms is Ronan; he's one today."

"Why are you marching?"

"We're tired of trying to find safety at night under the freeway."

"How long have you been...?"

"A few months after he was born. His father... well..."

"Relatives? Nearby?"

Suzanna shook her head, readjusted her grasp of the baby and was quickly lost, consumed by the on-going movement of humanity.

Matilda leaned over and held the microphone in front of a man, his hands propelling the wheels of his wheelchair. "What's your name and why are you in the march today?"

"I'm Piltdown, because the government says I don't exist, never did. So, I don't deserve to be here. But I'm human. I am here. And I need housing. I can't go on like this."

"What is the solution?" Matilda pressed.

"Government owes us all housing, happiness, and healthy lives. That's what I say to your microphone. Can it bring these things about?"

Matilda looked at Piltdown, at his chair, at the camera, then turned away, covered her face, and cried openly.

Recovering, she approached a bearded old man carrying a sign that read "Remember Mike Hawthorne." She introduced herself and asked for the man's name.

"Sun and Stars," he told her.

"Who was or is Mike Hawthorne?"

"A role model. He said he hated all those other people with houses and apartments, but we all knew it was his way of expressing compassion and even love for those who were not one of us, one of us homeless."

"Here today?"

Sun and Stars pointed upward, his gaze going toward heaven. He smiled and said, "Mike's lucky. He finally found a home."

CHAPTER FIVE:
THE COUSIN

Her private office door was always open, inviting anyone on her staff who wanted to present a fresh idea, perhaps offer a solution, or convey some uplifting news to come in and speak to her. "Something, please, some new idea, some solution," she would implore her staff during their Monday morning meetings. This morning, in reaction to the marchers' continual slogan yelling from outside as reported on the television, Angelika Murphy called out, "Josh, turn off that TV! It makes it all worse."

In the resultant silence, Ms. Murphy stood, ready to greet the youngish and yet serious media reporter being shown into her office by one of her staff assistants. "From New York, Mr. White, welcome," was her cordial greeting expressed in her deeper-than-typical early-thirty-something female lilt. "I'm Angelika."

"Allen," he said, shaking her hand in a formal I've-crossed-the-continent-from-Manhattan-style greeting. "Thank you for the opportunity to meet you and learn about this new and unique position you hold in Regional government circles." As he spoke, he took mental note of the nameplate on her desk, "Angelika Murphy, Multi City and County Housing Coordinator." He recorded in his mind her two framed academic degrees on the wall. They accredited two PhDs in City Planning, one from Oxford and the other from Stanford. Looking around as journalists are trained to do, he saw that a map covering one wall of her large office was of the many cities, counties, and unincorporated areas constituting the Region of Yerba Buena, which was his assignment to research and report upon as well as to do a human interest article about the woman in charge of this vast area's regional planning and oversight of real estate development.

Of course, he took quick mental note for his article as to Angelika's fashionable attire. When interviewing a prominent woman, a reporter always had to tell what she was wearing; whereas if it was a male, it was assumed he was attired in a suit and tie, or a turtleneck or whatever was the latest male style trend. Often the male sartorial comment was omitted. But here was a woman. Pert, he judged Angelika, and with an assertive appearance. Yes, she must be a strong woman to have been awarded this powerful job. Public records, which he had researched ahead of time, revealed that her position paid well into six figures, with a host of vacation perks, health, and retirement benefits.

The dazzler on her ring finger caused Allen some surprise, diverting him from his interview plan, as he blurted, "You're married!" At her nod, he asked in proper order about her husband and if they had any children. Thinking fast, he dropped the usual and intrusive curious "yet" part of his question.

Angelika motioned for the two of them to sit at the small table positioned to have a view across Yerba Buena. He asked to take several pictures of her, to which she agreed, as she replied, "Yes, my husband Peter is with a start-up tech company. I'm still trying to understand what they're doing, but whatever it is, they just raised 500 mill venture capital money on their second round of what he termed "mezzanine" financing." She shrugged her shoulders. "You asked about kids?" She shook her head. "No time."

He asked, "Will there ever be time?"

She laughed. "Maybe when the world stops whirling at break-neck speed. But let me ask you, Allen, do any of us really want to bring children into this world? I mean, apart from, say, the biological drive? Think from a societal point of view."

His turn to nod, perhaps in agreement or wanting to comment, but he was not the one being interviewed, she was. A handsome male assistant brought two cups of green tea. Allen smiled at him and said to her, "Well, I'm gay, but my partner and I have talked about adopting." He appended, "At some time. But living in Manhattan as we do, having a kid to look after? We just don't know. He's with a publishing company, so we both work, and nannies are not cheap. I mean, the costs… we've looked into it a bit."

She reflected, "Maybe adopting is different from having."

Allen thought he agreed. Existing, as opposed to hoping. "Quote you on that?"

Nodding, she said, "As to your article, Allen," she began, "we all—including you and your magazine—know the story, have already defined some aspects of the problem and are, like us here, searching for solutions. We are all seeking a light at the end of the population and employment and housing tunnel. We need your help to spread the story. Maybe if enough people read about the nationwide— indeed worldwide—homeless problem and feel the angst, the stress, the need for help, someone, somewhere will come up with something."

Allen nodded as he set up his laptop on the table and got ready to ask his planned questions, but Angelika cut him off, "I know the problem. You know the problem. Those marchers out there on the streets are first-hand experiencing the problem, but I dare say none of them has a solution any more than you or I."

The reporter pointed to her title. Smiling, he asked, "One hundred and five cities and unincorporated areas set up the Region of your jurisdiction. All this vast Region of Yerba Buena is under the control of your agency. How does that make you feel? Powerful?"

"Like Moses with no Red Sea to part." Angelika laughed and, caught in a moment of mutual silence, dabbed her eyes with a tissue.

Interrupting the mood, her cell played "Home on the Range." She looked at the device's screen, said an "excuse me," tapped a button, and said, "Are you in the march?" Her nod suggested the caller was. "Need anything later on?" Silence as she listened. "Love," she said finally, and added, "I do, and I know, Cuz. Do you have a place for tonight?" Silence. " Under the freeway on the I-80 onramp." She gritted her teeth and said, "Come by tomorrow... early, so you can use the shower and cook your special oatmeal." The cell conversation ended with a "love you." With an apologetic tone in her voice, she told the reporter, "Stuart, he's my first cousin."

"Homeless?"

She nodded. "He is. 'Fraid so, though he has a job. Can't find a place to live. Even if he could, he can't afford any rentals on his own or even sharing with a buddy, let alone buying something. Forget that! Not with his student debt and car loan payments hanging over him. I mean, do you know what the median cost is of a home is in the Region?" Angelika didn't wait for his guess. "It's close to one million dollars. And then you get into a bidding war with a bunch of other buyers, so my friends with sufficient income and down payment tell me. And do you know what the typical asking rent for even a studio is?" She didn't wait for him to shake his head in a negative gesture. "It's two thousand five hundred a month, and that's just for a studio of maybe 600 square feet at the most."

Allen made notes and then asked, "Tell me, what is your cousin's background?"

"Two degrees, one in English literature, the other something to do with experimental teaching. Was married, but they broke up. They couldn't find a nest satisfactory to her, as she wanted to have a baby." Angelika was silent, reflecting for a moment. Then she said, "How many? How many lives are askew from what used to be considered society's norm? School, marriage, a house, family—more or less in that order. How many households are not being formed, or are falling apart?"

"How many are there? Homeless, I mean. Say, here in Yerba Buena? In the metropolitan area, the Region, your Region? That is, in your area of real estate planning responsibility? And how many in the state?"

Angelika gestured at one of the walls in her office showing a map of the Region. She said, "When each of the cities and areas in the region voted to centralize their planning and turn it over to our new agency—that was four years ago—take the local politics out of the loop and think in terms of jobs, transportation, and housing for everyone in this magnet area of advanced technology, where people from all over the world were coming to apply for jobs and pursue technological creativity, we devised a dedicated project to count the homeless."

"How'd that work out?"

"We hired a group of actors from several live theater performing groups to impersonate the homeless, costumed them, and told them to move among the homeless, pretending to be homeless, all the while counting those men and women and children living on the streets."

"And?"

Angelika said, "Over a week, these actors counted a total of almost two hundred thousand people. It was, of course, not a true census, but gave us—for planning purposes—reliable estimates."

The reporter took notes. "That's daunting."

Angelika nodded. "But we weren't able to count the homeless who were sleeping in their cars, huddled down so as not to be detected. Nor did we make an effort to count those riding around all night in a bus or on a subway train."

Allen commented in a tone of disbelief, "Sleeping in parked cars?"

"And in old discarded RVs, trailers—parked on some side street, much to the consternation of nearby residents." She looked hard at Allen and said, "And then you have the sanitation problem. Cars and old RVs and tents—none of them have facilities. One group of well-meaning people took it upon themselves to set up porta potties in a little park. They arranged for 10 of the freestanding toilets. That was in an area with more than 1,000 homeless living nearby on the streets, in cars, in old SUVS, or whatever. Then came the question of servicing the potties. That's not cheap. Soon the local group lost interest as the demands for more and more money confronted them."

"Where do the homeless park these cars?"

"Anyplace they can find to park overnight legally without being harassed by the police or set upon by vagrants and robbed or, maybe worse. Neighbors are always complaining, afraid they'll get mugged on their own doorstep, you know. So the police may come and roust the homeless and their cars, off to who knows where."

Allen nodded, made more notes and then asked, "Some time ago, even in the New York papers, there was a story about a passenger ship that had docked at one of the ports here that was accepting passengers, but of course, was not going to sail anywhere; it planned to stay moored and provide housing."

"Yes, that solution was tried, but a host of problems surfaced, and the idea was soon scrubbed."

"What happened?"

"One problem was sufficient shore-side parking for residents, so the ship owners discovered they were in violation of both the zoning and building codes. That's an example of how what might seem like a logical plan running afoul of local laws and regulations. For example, another question had to do with which law enforcement agency had jurisdiction over the ship and its residents? The Coast Guard punted. The sheriff's department said, "not us," and that left the city police, who distanced themselves. Fearing a lawless environment, with the safety of inhabitants in jeopardy, raising their liability insurance rates through the roof, the ship's owners pulled the plug, and the ship, devoid of residents, sailed away into the fog."

"And I suppose you'll laugh if I ask you about houseboats as a doable solution for the homeless. I mean, there's lots of water around here—bays and rivers." From my plane, I saw houseboats floating in a couple of harbors."

Angelika nodded. "Yes, some rich people have suggested that. But if you've ever looked into owning a houseboat yourself, you'll answer that question quite quickly. It's as expensive as building a house, and you have problems of getting utilities, plus the threat of sudden king tides and storm turbulence."

Angelika continued, "But the ship experience we just talked about highlights this whole area of legal problems. Each of our cities has laws about being homeless, some having to do with sanitation, but most discriminate against people on the streets. These laws fall under the broad label of 'Anti-Homeless Architectural Features'."

"How do such laws affect the homeless?"

"Well, I suppose you could blame it on the architectural lobby."

"How so?"

"Angelika reflected a moment and said, "Architects don't want their creative designs blemished with either debris—litter—or homeless people and their tents and dogs blocking the view of their precious architectural statement or preventing people from entering their creation. Both situations would discourage regular folks, those who are employed and have homes, from entering the building, or even walking past it. They would choose a different route, or go somewhere else. The building owners would be upset and so would the tenants in the building wanting to attract customers."

"Can you give me an example?" Allen readied his computer as he listened.

"One city law calls for no loitering within 100 feet of buildings. If someone does, then the police come and haul them off." Another law prohibits sleeping bags or blankets within 100 feet, and certainly no tents on the lawns or sidewalks near buildings. Anyone caught with a blanket or a sleeping bag walking near such buildings and who doesn't have a permanent address nearby can be arrested, jailed, and fined, even deported by Immigration authorities, who are likely to be summoned to the scene."

"How many cities have such laws?"

"Almost every city has some laws along those lines." She looked at Allen, hoping he had gotten the legal message before she added,

"But the real problems are in the categories of personal safety and hygiene."

Allen waited for her to explain, his eyebrows raised.

She said, "Streets were not built for living, obviously. There's no sanitation for people living on the streets. We bring in some porta potties, but they get overloaded and sometimes, in a wave of rage from disgruntled homeless, they get tipped over. Streets weren't built with showers, nor were freeway on-ramps. Therein lies the largest number of citizen and local government complaints, producing more prejudices against the homeless. But what do people expect the homeless to do? And what do the homeless expect people to do for them?"

They sat in silence, Allen typing words onto his keyboard. Angelika stood and looked out her wide office window at Yerba Buena stretching below her and reaching to the horizon in all directions. She said, "You know, I forgot to tell you about another solution that has been tried. In fact, it is still being attempted."

He stood, stretched, flexed his fingers, and said, "Go on, please."

"Abandoned warehouses is the category. There are some. They're vacant, of course, often near one of the port facilities. Homeless break in—although sometimes the doors are open or unlocked, and they set up their tents, or cardboard houses, or whatever. In one old building a group of artists got together and set up their sleeping bags and canvases, or whatever medium they were using, and went to work, living and working there."

"What did you do about that?"

"When we realized the fire department hadn't made any inspections, we found out that the fire departments in the Region are short of personnel—I mean, the firemen and women can't afford to live here, even with subsidies from the cities. They still can't find housing. So, building inspections suffer. Fires break out, and the response time is often tardy."

She sat back down and looked at Allen and expressed with emotion, "And in this one particular building an awful fire did break out. It was terrible." She shook her head and looked away. "Just last week. They're still retrieving bodies out of that morbid furnace. Artists were trapped. The building had no fire extinguishers, no exit signs, exit doors were locked. It was just the worst thing possible."

"How many died?"

27

"At last count, 55. And they expect the count will go higher."

Allen asked, "You mentioned that police and firemen are having trouble finding housing in the cities where they work?"

"Yes, many of them commute for miles. In fact, one policeman was spending so much time commuting from his home up in the foothills of the Sierra Nevada Mountains, 150 miles away, that he fell asleep one day and, driving to work, went over the cliff. And, of course, he…"

Allen added this bit of information to his notes as she added, "The problem is not limited to police and firemen; it includes city workers, office workers, utility repair people, and so on and on and on."

In a hushed voice, she added, "God knows what'll happen in the Region if we get another major earthquake—these buildings haven't been inspected to determine if the legislated upgrades have been installed. We can't hire the needed inspectors. Several years ago, the state legislature passed a law…" And her voice trailed off.

Allen said, "I want to go back to the story of the policeman commuting from such a long distance. Let me ask you this: "Can't there be set up a commute system—high speed bullet trains, for example, coming in from these more remote areas of the state, so that people can find housing and live at these distances while still getting to work here?"

She said, "Do you know what it would take to build a series— even just one—high speed train line?"

"I don't."

"Well, by the time you'd weave your way through the approval processes with the state, the federal government, each county, each city in the path of the proposed right-of-way, prepare and file your documents, hold hearings on the required environmental impact report, and field lawsuits from people fighting the eminent domain game, hell will have frozen over. This, Allen, is not China where the government just does things. Here, every person for miles around gets to kibbitz on any project, give their two cents, and then sue to stop the project."

"I guess it's called democracy'"

"I guess," she said, and they sat in silence for a while. "But not for the immigration authorities."

"How do you mean?"

A certain number of homeless are illegal immigrants. They may have jobs, earn money, have families, but their visas have expired or they never had one."

"What do they do?"

"Evade the authorities while they go to see an immigration attorney and try to be become legal, hopefully apply for citizenship. That is, if they aren't deported in the meantime."

"Where do they hide from the immigration police?"

"Used to be in churches."

"Not any more?"

"Well, some churches have set up beds for homeless, and that includes some illegal immigrants, I suppose. But sanctuary in a sacred facility is no longer guaranteed. In fact, one church in their basement had set up a lot of facilities for homeless, and then there was a raid by a combination of police, firemen and immigration. Everyone was arrested, including the priest, for harboring criminals."

Allen kept typing and then looked up to ask, "Angelika, could you please describe your job for me? And also can you outline the mission of your department."

"Simple in one sense. We're the planning authority for the megalopolis—the entire Region. We process development requests, issue building permits, and conduct follow-up inspections to assure that construction meets the uniform building code."

"Well then, under these circumstances, there must be a lot of applications for new buildings?"

"Not really. You see, Allen, almost all of the land in the Region has been built-out. Oh, there are some proposed demolitions to be replaced with taller structures, for offices and housing. And, given the laws governing air rights, there are applications to add floors to existing buildings."

"How does that work?"

"Under the legislation that created my agency, each building in the region was awarded air rights equal to the height of the existing structure, providing that the structural integrity of the proposed development can be certified by structural engineers."

"Like if I have a one-story house, I can add a second floor?"

Angelika nodded. "And if you have a 10-story building, you could add 10 more floors." She went on, "These air rights can be bought and sold. So, in theory if you buy enough air rights, you could build a high rise of infinite height. "But, of course, we would not approve such a thing."

"What about people going farther out into the countryside to find housing," Allen asked.

"Yes, some do, and our staff has talked to them. They can go south of Gilroy to Hollister, or east out into the Central Valley past Tracy to little towns like Newman, or search up north to Cloverdale and towns like that. There's no trains… oh, some buses, but they get caught in the traffic, too. Either way, their commutes border on 3 hours… that's just one-way—makes six hours a day commuting. Now, after that, even if you're young like us, how much residual energy by midweek or the end of the week have you got left to apply to doing your job?"

Allen commented, "And I thought Manhattan commutes were long and arduous." Changing the subject, he asked, "How many employees do you have?"

"More than 500, in 10 offices scattered around the Region."

"Unionized?"

"Most, Public Employees."

"And a Board of Directors?"

"Yes, actually at last count, 100 civic-minded citizens."

"Isn't that an unwieldy size for you to report to?"

"Yes, it takes me and my staff a lot of time and effort to keep them all informed, of course." She showed him a large chart and said, "Our organizational plan is patterned after the Metropolitan Museum of Art in Manhattan."

The reporter chuckled. "That doesn't seem to be working too well, so I understand."

Angelika said, "This here's the West, not the East Coast. We're different."

"How so?"

"We think for ourselves here. My region is somewhat like the Delphi Oracle, the center of the world when it comes to new thinking, new ideas, and creativity. We deal with mental challenges, and are not mired down in social status and class privileges." She thought about her statement and said, "Don't quote me on that." She pleaded, "Please." Then she added, "Even so, we still can't agree on how to solve the overriding problem of the homeless."

Allen asked if he could quote her.

"Sure, the last part."

One other question: "You said most all of the land here is developed? Except maybe for tidelands at the edge of the big bay."

"The environmentalists wont allow any changes to those large tidal areas. Besides, with global warming, the sea level is going to rise, and we'd have to truck in mountains of fill dirt to combat the rising ocean and then create enough of a foundation to support buildings. I mean, there are not enough trucks to bring in enough dirt to raise the soil levels high enough. Worse, foundations would be unstable from a structural point of view. So, those areas and the Bay itself are off limits." She stood and made sweeping arm gestures over those areas on her wall map. "Yes, Allen, it's all developed, except…"

She asked if he wanted more tea. He nodded and the male assistant soon returned. She went on, "You see, the trouble is, if you look at the in-migration into this region from all over our country and from overseas as a result of all the new jobs being created here, you'll see that the immigrants are arriving three times as fast as housing units can be built for them. Except, that there are so few new housing projects today. I mean, almost none. Except…"

"Immigrants from where?"

"Everywhere. Asia, Africa, the Middle East, Europe."

"Why do they keep coming?"

"Jobs. Opportunities. A lot more money than they can earn back home, plus the promise of a lifestyle better than anything offered in their native lands."

"Who are the people offering these jobs, these opportunities?"

Angelika produced a table showing figures from recent venture capital investments in companies, both new and recently formed. "These figures are for the last year we have data. The grand total comes to more than 10 billion dollars of risky venture capital money put up by investment companies in my Region to start new ventures or finance ones just getting underway. That is many times that of Boston, New York and other major cities, where most capital comes from, combined. For us, that means a lot of new jobs, exciting jobs, challenging jobs, and multiple chances to make a lot of money for young people from all over the world who migrate here. As a result, they are coming here in droves, wanting to live here. But there's no housing for them, or very little, except for the super wealthy. In increasing numbers, the ones with money are buying up available houses in middle to upper price brackets."

"Lots of people from other countries." His observation confirmed her statement. She nodded as Allen made more notes.

Finishing, he thanked Angelika. "Now I must fly back to low-tech New York." He chuckled. He was about to leave when she tugged at his sleeve and said, "If you want to experience these immigrants firsthand, come with me now and we'll cruise Valencia Street. But first, I'll tell you one more bit of information you should know."

"A question I forgot to ask?"

"You might say so. It is most important to a possible solution to our homeless question."

"And it is?"

Angelika went to the wall map and pointed to a large land area devoid of roads and development. The vacant space was colored green, indicating a forest or a natural area devoid of human imprint—the only such area of any note anywhere on the map. "Look here," she said, "here is enough land to solve our housing problem, enough land to build sufficient small housing projects— even those factory-built 'tiny houses' for those who are today's homeless."

"Well then, why don't you approve development and get under way?"

"The owners covet their own exclusive high-level housing plans, so they simply won't sell, so we understand."

Allen thought for a moment and asked, "What about using eminent domain to acquire the land? Wouldn't such a lawsuit be for the public good, that being to provide housing for homeless? After all, aren't you a public agency, really the government? And governments everywhere in this country have eminent domain rights, don't they?"

Angelika smiled, "You may have the theoretical solution to print in your article. But theory and practice don't always mesh."

"You're saying that eminent domain is a complex legal matter?"

She nodded. "I have a complex job."

"And I have a complex article to write."

"Now, on to Valencia Street while you think about that" Angelika said. They left her office and made for the train connection to the Valencia Street station.

*   *   *

Together, as the evening dusk darkened toward night, they walked along Valencia Street, dodging hordes of young people. They passed bar after wine bar after bistro, each one brimming with people.

"These are your techies," Angelika said. "Let's go into this bistro and listen to the conversations." Inside they elbowed their way to the bar amid the gender mix of young women and young men.

"Nobody over 50," the reporter observed.

"Thirty-five's more likely the oldest," she said.

"Where are they from?"

"Keokuk, Iowa, Kokomo, Indiana, Mumbai, India, anywhere in China, somewhere in Japan, and Philippines, you name it. As is their right as human beings, they are seeking the brass ring of social media, starting up new tech companies, seeking jobs in existing companies, running existing companies, many sleeping on the streets, all for themselves, their families here and back home, whether that home is in this country or elsewhere in the world."

Allen listened to snippets of conversation and, puzzled, asked, "You know, I understand the words, but their sentences don't make any sense to me."

Angelika said, "It's the vocabulary of the future. We here are on the horizon of civilization, in my opinion. I don't know what they're talking about either. Several times I stopped to ask some of them and gotten a friendly explanation, which I didn't fully comprehend. But I can tell you it is about changing the world for the better. It is about their ideas of improving civilization, and maybe making money for each of them while doing so. It's about new ideas, socially, and technologically."

They shook hands and she bid goodbye to Allen for his flight back east. "I'll email you a draft of my article for your critique," he told her as he left.

On Allen White's flight back east, Angelika assumed he would continue making notes, composing his feature article. She was glad for his visit, glad she had a major journalist to tell the story of the homeless in the Region. Upon his arrival, she visualized his airport taxi taking him to a chic West Side co-op or condominium home. She wondered if he would ignore the homeless sleeping on the street near the entrance to his building? Once inside, would his portion of the home (he said had a partner) be filled with mementos of his journalistic career? She could almost see his framed journalistic awards and photographs covering his "me-wall." Surely he had a "me-wall." Didn't you have to be a bit narcissistic to be a journalist? She had always thought of it as a career where you were subject to criticism, both from your editors and from your readers, as you competed with fellow journalists for space in print or time on the tube? Maybe she'd be attracted to a journalist, that is if she were to do it all over again, meaning the replay of the mating dance.

Ah, she reflected, the comfort of being home. Would he feel it within himself? Would he remember the homeless of the Region he had just visited? The marchers? The statistics she had given him? Would her cousin, for example, remain in his report's story? Once in his Manhattan sanctuary, would Allen feel safe from the world outside, safe from the world's progress, safe from the unknowns of the future, yes, and safe from change? That is, she speculated, until the following morning when the sun would come up over Central Park. Then it might suddenly dawn on him that changes in society were coming fast and furious. Would he realize society's lack of personal and community resources for dealing with change? Yes, Angelika thought as she left her office to head home to hopefully see Peter, her high-tech husband.

Her house. Their house—a mini mansion on a half acre lot. They could afford it, did afford it, and would continue to afford it—the mortgage payments, the property taxes, the insurance—fire, earthquake, flood, wind, liability—plus the physical upkeep of the property, including painting, and the continual landscaping maintenance. Damn, she thought, how much did they spend on installing that state-of-the-art drip irrigation system that saved gallons of water every day, so they could brag to their friends and neighbors they were "green" compliant? Indeed, the long list of money going out of their checking account rolled over in her mind. All that money! But what was money for, anyway, she asked herself, if not to spend and enjoy its fruits? Wasn't that what the venture capitalists were contemplating for their checkbooks when they put 500 mill into her husband's company? Well, of course, it was because he and it were on the cusp of the breakthroughs in technology—right there on the cutting edge of the future. Their investment returns would be astronomical, as had been explained to her by bright young people

knowledgeable about the financing of the future.

It was then that she recalled earlier that day catching a glimpse on the TV of the marchers waving their placards—before Josh followed her instruction to turn the thing off. One of the placards she saw that one of the marchers was carrying read: *Demolish Mansions; Build Housing for Us.*

Angelika felt a tinge of guilt as she punched in the code that unlocked her entry door. As she entered, she surveyed her up-to-the-latest designer-decorated home. Everything in the house was so tony, so cool, so magazine. Five mill, at least, she estimated. As she moved lithely about amidst the chic interior, Angelika wondered why she didn't feel the contentment promised to her.

CHAPTER SIX:
THE BAVARIAN CLUB

The many styles of architecture had come to America from Europe down through the years, arriving in waves de jour. Beaux Arts was no exception. Following an earlier infatuation with Greek Revival, then English Georgian, interspersed with American Federal, and later by Spanish Colonial, this earlier French school advocated paired columns topped with stately capitals separating inspiring arches, the combination suggesting an impressive and enduring strength for the building and for the architect, as well— accolades that promised to transcend the centuries.

Since the German Bauhaus school didn't really develop much in architecture, sticking as it did to art and design, the Yerba Buena Bavarian Club chose the French Beaux Arts style for its stately headquarters building in the center of the extensive business district. By now its architectural statement had offered itself to the skyline for well over a hundred years. Back then, the German immigrant architect, Adolph Vogel, in envisioning the multi-storied building, was infatuated with Berlin's Brandenburg Gate. And so he had gone to work designing his New World masterpiece.

The result seemed to many to be visual intimidation. And if an observer was ever invited inside the building, which wasn't likely, his or her—well, not a her—emotional experience would verify the initial reaction to seeing the intimidating interior of the Bavarian Club for the first time, and even thereafter. Upstairs were tucked away small intimate private dining rooms where members could bring prominent male guests and, on very special rare occasions, approved female guests. The focal point of each room was an oil painting done by a notable artist, the work elegantly framed and subtly lighted. Velvet drapes softened the clinking of glasses, and candles augmented the subdued retro-fitted electric lighting to the point of suggesting a calming mesmerism.

One floor was devoted to a large dining hall for less intimate daily lunches, dinners, chamber music concerts, and piano recitals. On another level were private bedrooms for members who chose not to return home to their respective mansions for the evening, for one marital reason or another, and for club members of affiliated clubs in other metropolitan areas around the world to occupy when visiting Yerba Buena. Even the elevators were adorned with framed etchings of yesteryear's engravers. The hallways displayed sculptures of bronze and marble atop ornate pedestals.

This midday, inside the fourth floor walnut-paneled inner sanctum reading room of this exclusive all-male club—you weren't blessed with a membership invitation unless your father, grandfather, state governor, celebrated celebrity, or prominent politician was or had been a member and, in addition, you received endorsements from five members in good standing—the counter revolution to the marchers outside was under way. The opposition was not displayed with placards, not with calls for justice, but instead with conversations as to the inalienable rights of property owners. As one listened to the expressions, there was evident defiance of the populist sentiment being expressed by the tens of thousands of homeless and homeless sympathizers marching through the streets down below.

Listening to the club members and catching glimpses from the fourth floor window, Chief Club Steward Mario Mondragon reflected that it had been almost 15 years since the day he had become the head steward. Before his promotion, he'd been employed for five years, first in the kitchen as a dishwasher, then as a dining hall waiter and now, on a daily basis, he was circulating amongst the elite of the club, privileged to listen to their banter, their competitive chatter, their establishment wisdom, and their ethnic, racial, and gender prejudices.

As he, too, surveyed the marchers, Mario thought back. It had been some twenty years since he'd found his way across the border of the Rio Grande east of Ciudad Juarez and El Paso and slowly, avoiding detection, made his way through Texas and on to Yerba Buena. Once in the city of his destination, he'd sent for his wife and two young children. They'd followed his route, soon joining him. His wife, enterprising, had opened a Mexican restaurant in the right location near the Bavarian Club. Her enterprise had been helped to grow and prosper through Mario's subtle promotion among club members of her authentic Northern Mexican cuisine. Over time, her good cooking had endeared her menu specialties to a clientele of Yerba Buenians, whether or not they were members of the Bavarian Club.

To the members of the Bavarian Club, he was always Mario, and nothing else. No last name. Mario doubted few of them knew or even cared about his family name, his background, or his political beliefs. He brought them drinks, and they tipped him, many times generously. They were seldom rude to him unless he accidentally spilled their drink, which had happened only once, and that was when one of them—intentionally, he had thought—bumped into him in what he sensed was a display of overt ethnic prejudice.

To him the members, each and every one, were always addressed as "Mister." He learned that they each had pet nicknames, and it was in that unique nomenclature that he thought about them when they placed their drink orders with him. He'd remember their order by their nicknames. Today, as he looked their way from the side of the reading room, he remained alert for their wishes. From his position, he could watch "Goody" Herbst, who he had learned was the chairman of the club's board of directors. "Goody" was looking out of a fourth floor window watching the demonstrators and shaking his head in disapproval. Catching the attention of "Flowers," a fellow member, "Goody" pointed to the marchers. He said in what Mario thought was a judgmental tone, "Those people have plenty of housing available to them if they'd just get off their asses and do a little looking around. There're lots of places listed for rent or for sale in those weekly throwaway newspapers they all read."

"And online, as well, so my barber tells me," "Flowers" said, adding, "Pricey, though. My barber's looked because his son needs a place to stay. Right now his son is in an SRO."

"What's an SRO?"

"Short for Standing Room Only, so I understand. Maybe 100 square feet at most, he tells me, but no kitchen, hopefully a place to piss. His son is paying $1,800 a month. The member went on, "You know, the trouble with those riff-raff marchers down there is that they are too caught up in causes, whether it's sexual, trans…, whatever it is, or political. Why don't they just get on the Internet, find jobs, and go to work or else help out in the family business like the rest of us did during our lifetimes?"

"I don't do that computer stuff," "Doggie" said. "I like to never had made it here this morning. My driver couldn't get within blocks of the club. The police had blocked off the streets for those marchers down there. So, he let me out, and I had to walk the rest of the way." He gestured at Mario waiting in the wings, "Mario, bring me a Scotch neat and a glass of ice water." To "Goody," he said, "You know, if we'd stop giving out free needles and providing all those free tents and community shelters… that's why these homeless people come here from all over the country. Do away with the freebies, and they'll all leave and go back where they came from."

"Yeah, that's what my friends tell me," said "Loopy," a tall double-breasted-suited member, directing his next remark to the others, "But someone tell me why are those demonstrators complaining about gender? Whatever happened to accepted gender roles?"

"Whatever happened to gender?" came a reply from "Cap'n". "That four-month cruise my wife and I were just on, why it was all couples, regular men and normal women. Ah, how many… oh, 2,000 at least regular American couples on board. And at 20 grand a passenger… we had great staterooms, free drinks, entertainment…"

"Shhh," hissed "Sharpie" from behind his *Financial Times*. "This is a reading room. Silence here, gentlemen. Club rules."

Nobody seemed to heed his edict, for another member, "Lucky," said, "No gender confusion on that cruise ship my wife and I took. Six weeks all around the Middle East. Tours of each of the ports we called at. There were lots of couples on board, and lots of entertainment. Lots of food, too, and you should have seen those cute waitresses, hear the music, and watch the dancers every night. Yeah, we had free drinks, too, any time you wanted one. Most of the passengers were walking around blotto a good deal of the time." And he laughed.

Continuing to look down at the marchers, "Goody" commented, "Why don't they join the army or the navy—that way, they'd get shelter, jobs, money—I mean, that's what most of us did those years ago in the Korean War, or Viet Nam."

"Yes, we were patriots," said a tall bewhiskered member known as "Whiskers." "We fought for our country… well, I mean, instead I went to divinity school so I could preach the word of God to those going off to war and who might not come back."

"That way, 'Whiskers,' you could escape the draft," "Flowers" said and laughed. His remark was in jest, Mario thought, or at least he presumed "Flowers" intended it to be so.

"Whiskers" scowled back and, pointing down toward the street, said, "What are those malcontents doing for their country? Yes, patriotism—"

"—Is it in the Bible? Patriotism, I mean."

"Lots of things are in the Bible," "Whiskers" said, adding, "In my church there's a men's group. Every Sunday we hand out Bibles among the homeless. For them to read, I mean."

"What's their reaction to that?"

"They thank us, of course. For the most part, they're polite. But then one of them told me that their tents don't have reading lights. Another said he'd rather have fish or wine, like in the Bible."

"Listen," "Goody" said, addressing his fellow members, while still watching the march below, "My son-in-law's an attorney for some of those homeless people out there. How they can afford to pay his fee I don't know—"

"—Probably a benefactor, some liberal asshole," commented "Cap'n", who added, "I agree with "Flowers" here. We'd save a lot of city money by just giving each of 'em bus tickets back to Nevada or wherever they came from. Then they'd all leave, and when they got back where they came from they'd tell their friends to stay put because there's no free drugs or needles or food or anything for them here anymore."

"Goody" took his eyes off the marchers, turned and directly addressed his fellow club members. "Guys, my son-in-law tells me he is working up a lawsuit against us." All of a sudden he had their undivided attention. He continued, "When it is filed, his law firm will be coming after us... each and everyone of us... naming us in the suit as officers and directors of the Bavarian Club."

"Why us as individuals?"

"Because, 'Goody' explained, we're the governing board of the Bavarian Club, and our club has owned for more than a century this stately old building and the land under it. But what's a bigger prize for them—that is, my son-in-law and his lawyer wife—is our large tract of undeveloped land, the biggest piece of raw land anywhere within commuting distance of Yerba Buena."

"Ah, yes," "Doggie" said, reflecting, "our own private forest where we hold our summer high jinks while we live in tents out there in Mother Nature at home among old growth redwood trees."

"Well, never fear, my friends," "Goody" assured them, "that forest is our club's land. Goes back to our benefactor and founder, Barron Wilhelm von Herzog." He gestured at an oversized framed portrait of the Baron, who was sternly looking down at each of them. The members rose and offered a serious salute to the Baron as Mario brought "Goody" his Scotch, serving it from off a sterling silver tray with an engraved image of the baron's likeness peering up through the glass ice cube container on the tray's surface.

"Yes, it's our club's land," "Doggie" reassured everyone. "And we on the board have our little plan to divide a portion of it up among we long-term members on the board, so we can build our palatial homes on our respective 20-acre plots. It'll be homes for each of our families—our sons and daughters and grandchildren and... on and on... homes... estates to enjoy forever... in perpetuity."

Nods from the others, and then a barrage of gestures toward Mario to bring more drinks. Mario headed for his nearby bar and promptly returned, a yo-yo on a string, arriving just as the comment came, "'Goody,' how do we get to this son-in-law of yours? To dissuade him, make him come to his senses."

"Jeremy? Jeremy Dean—my daughter's husband. They both graduated from law school at Boalt. But we still talk. I don't know the attraction between them. She's conservative—gets it from me, of course, after all, my late wife and I raised her—but he's as liberal as Lenin. You know, for some reason—I think she's put him up to it—he's asked me about becoming a member of our club. My formal invitation to join is what he seeks. I guess it's for business reasons... get more clients for him, if he has access to members in these halls."

"Members who can pay the monthly bills," joked "Doggie." "And you're going to help him with the application fee?"

'Flowers' said, "I'm told a hundred thou is a lot of money for some of those people out there." He pointed to the marchers below.

"Goody" said, "He is my only daughter's husband." He sipped his scotch. "After their graduation, she asked me for money for a house. Jeremy's from a broken home somewhere around Oil City—"

"—That scrubby town near Bakersfield?"

"Goody" nodded. "I told them, as I did, they would have to earn the money first, so they could afford to buy a home and qualify for the mortgage on their own merits. And pay the real estate taxes and the insurance and keep it up. But he told me his FICO score is shit, so forget that, he said it in a tone I felt was disrespectful of my position in the community."

"Doggie" said, "FICO scores are our friend. They protect lenders from the scumbags out there intent on ripping them off. I mean, your son-in-law may not be a scumbag, but FICO is our protection from all the other riff-raff." He pointed down, identifying the marchers on the street.

"Yes, those ne'er-do-wells in the march," "Goody" said, receiving the nods of the others in the reading room. "But, men, what we've really got to stop is the regional authority that wants to take away our land. I hear they're talking about relying on eminent domain to try to get it. Some woman heads the agency, I'm told."

"Her name's Angelika something or other," one said.

"Damn, another woman we've got to deal with. Daughters are one thing, but women in the work place, that's another matter. We're for sure, in our time, going to be headed for socialism. Say goodbye to private property, hard work, and the benefits we've all come to know and treasure, I'm telling you!"

Every man in the room raised his glass in salute, again, to the oil portrait of Baron Wilhelm von Herzog. "To his foresight," they proclaimed as they paid tribute in unison.

CHAPTER SEVEN:
ILLEGAL ALIENS

Mario was surprised when "Goody' approached and put his around his shoulders—a most unusual movement—and said, "Mario, how are your two boys doing in community college?"

"Ramon is studying computer science. And Renaldo is doing pre-law. He wants to be an immigration attorney and help our fellow Hispanics fight immigration and deportation and help them get citizenship."

"And how are you coming along on your family's citizenship applications? You know, ICE is cracking down."

Mario hesitated and looked away as tears came to his eyes. Slowly, he said, "My wife is trying to sell our restaurant. Were going to have to go back to Mexico, I'm afraid. All of my family... my sons, too."

Overhearing the head steward, "Flowers" said, "Hey, that's one way to cut down on the homeless among those marchers outside. Deport all the illegal aliens."

Mario recalled that "Flowers" had been the one who had nudged him into dropping the drink. In a violation of club protocol, Mario blurted out, "We immigrants are not, by any measurement, the homeless people you see down there on the streets. Most of us have jobs, housing, and good FICO scores." He looked chagrined, and promptly said, "I'm sorry, Mr. 'Goody,' I'm being disrespectful, Sir."

"Can your priest be of any help?"

"He's urging Ramon and Renaldo to quit school and join the military. He thinks it would expedite their citizenship applications. You know, we're all—my entire family, illegal. We never bothered to get citizenship... didn't realize its importance."

"Sorry," was all "Goody" could manage to say. Then he asked, "Have you consulted an immigration attorney?"

Mario nodded. "Two, as a mater of fact. Some do pro bono and one is a steady customer at my wife's restaurant."

"And?"

"No hope under the new laws, I'm afraid."

"Sanctuary in the church?"

"My priest is strict law and order."

"A sanctuary city around here?"

"Maybe, but only for a few days at best, so I'm told by others. The chef here in the club—he's from France, but a citizen—said he'd adopt our two boys, but the immigration attorney said it wouldn't hold up."

Mario was summoned by a club member and had to repeat his trip to the bar.

CHAPTER EIGHT:
THE GOOD SHIP ALGONQUIN

Back those many years ago during World War II, the Region's several deep-water harbors had been beehives of ship building activity. Merchant ships along with submarines had been built here by women who came to be known on patriotic posters as Rosie the Riveter. Other ships came and went, loading war goods for the Pacific Theatre of combat. While that was a long time ago, remnants of what went on during that world war remained today if one knew where to look. Many people did know, and lately many people did look. Especially if they were homeless. What they found were usable hideaways that had been abandoned, such as Coast Guard concrete bunkers, some still with roofs.

Others found, as did Jeremy Dean and his wife, Anna, the Algonquin, a vintage supply ship docked at an abandoned port facility that happened to be within commuting bike distance of the Court Houses of one of the nine counties that made up the Region.

Trouble was, even with their new living situation joining with other shipmates, Jeremy and Anna also needed a law office. After all, if one (or two) had been admitted to the State Bar and wanted to practice law, the prestige of an office was necessary. After they had claimed the last livable stateroom in the Algonquin and set up housekeeping, such as it was, they needed to resolve the office issue.

Fortunately, to accommodate a multitude of business demands, enterprising real estate developers were building office facilities that provided minimal space for a desk, computer connections, and Wi-Fi, while offering a respectable business address. Featured were communal reception areas where clients and business partners, for example, could be met and where conference tables and chairs were available for required formal meetings.

Jeremy and Anna took what savings they had and what small amount of funds they could borrow from his father-in-law (her father) and set up their legal practice, which they determined would focus on community issues.

CHAPTER NINE:
ROGER ROADHOUSE, REALTOR

His father, Roger Senior, had built a lot of single family homes in Boise, Idaho. With some financial success over the years, he had battled winter storms, frozen ground, and demanding buyers. He once told his son that homebuyers in Idaho were strong individuals, which made them demanding buyers. For instance, they would often require that he re-paint or re-carpet the house before they would close their purchase. Sometimes they would demand that he change the driveway location to the other side of the house to conform to the sun's habits, benefiting, they would say, from sunshine warming the property in the long winter months and melting the accumulated snow and ice on the driveway—but if the driveway was on the shaded side of the house, the sun would never melt the ice and snow, and they'd have to chip away at the stuff and shovel it themselves.

However, when his last group of houses failed to sell, Roger would tell about his father becoming disillusioned with the business. That was when Roger Senior decided to retire. After his father had moved to Southern California, it had been up to Roger Junior to study for his own real estate broker's exam so he could qualify for his Idaho license. Only then could he, on his own as an owner-broker, launch a campaign to sell all 10 houses in this, his father's last development.

After studying the situation of the houses, Roger realized that the buyer resistance lay in the location of the houses. Standing by them early one spring morning prior to holding open the model home for Sunday lookers, Roger quickly understood the reason for buyer resistance. For promptly at 6 AM on this early Sunday morning— with the Idaho Air National Guard practicing maneuvers at the Boise airport—jet fighter planes began to take off on a runway that, with their jets blasting, took them right over Roger's 10 houses. He found out after inquiring of the National Guard commander that these jets did their maneuvers every fourth Sunday morning at the same cruel wake-up time.

Roger adjusted to this situation, which he realized was a major deterrent to sales. Boise is not that big of a town, and word of the Air Force maneuvers spread among potential home buyers. Due to real estate broker regulations, they were required to advise prospective buyers of anything possibly adverse to their purchase, and jet fighters at six in the morning on certain Sundays was not the same as a sweet breeze blowing in the nearby cottonwood trees.

With focused effort on his part, which included effective advertising, plus price adjustments and attractive incentives, Roger found enough Air Force retirees as buyers—pilots who loved the commanding and exhilarating sound of jet planes taking off. To set the tone for his street of houses, Roger commissioned a sculptor to create a bronze replica of a jet plane lifting off. He positioned the artwork in a landscaped park at the entrance to his father's housing development. Months later, playing on the resultant pilot camaraderie, he closed the sale on the last house. And Roger headed for the warmer climate of Northern California.

Roger relied upon his Idaho real estate license to shorten the time period for qualifying for a California broker's license. Now licensed, he set up a desk and little office in the lobby of a prestigious 5-star hotel, offering to find homes for the super wealthy who had arrived in the area and who were staying at the luxury hotel.

One day while driving a prospective client, an executive for a technology company about to have its initial public stock offering, Roger was following a detour so he could show the executive a special house that he thought might fit his requirements. On this back road, they happened to pass a huge undeveloped piece of property that seemed to him to extend forever. "How could this be," he gestured at the land and asked himself out loud. "Given the housing shortage in the Yerba Buena Region?" His client shared the wonderment and, in the spirit of entrepreneurship, an enthusiasm for which they both felt a philosophical bonding, his client said, "You know, if I were you, I'd look into who owns this huge parcel of undeveloped land."

*   *   *

Roger did just that on his first day free of showing houses to the Region's incoming executives and techies. He went to the Yerba Buena Region's Planning Office and sought out the Recorder's office, where he spoke to the first available clerk. That was after quite a long wait as the office was crowded with other real estate agents, some of whom he had come to know.

Roger had identified the large parcel on a county map, so when his customer number came up and the County official was available to address Roger's query, he cited the parcel number and asked who owned the property. The agent responded without even looking the land up in a ledger book or on the Region's new computer system (Roger knew they were converting the old manual records to digital), by telling Roger, "You're the fifteenth person asking about that parcel this week."

Roger showed his surprise as the clerk, whose nametag read "Rosylyn" continued, "I tell them all the same and nothing ever happens, at least so far as we here in the County know about any development application."

"And what is it you tell them?"

"I'll give you same information." Rosylyn, seemingly by now from memory of having given the information out so many times, wrote on a piece of paper, "Homeward Bound Enterprises, c/o Gladstone & Cornwallis, Esquire, Box 6, Nassau, Bahamas."

Roger stood for a moment, digesting the information, then asked, "Who pays the property taxes? And are they current?"

"You must ask the County Assessor," Rosylyn advised.

"But you know?" Roger hinted.

She smiled and said, "I have been asked that several times before today."

"And your answer was?"

"The property taxes are always paid on time. And, I can tell you, the bill is huge. The land has been assessed at a high figure."

"But who pays the property tax bill?" Roger added, "And there has to be fire danger there in the summer when the natural grasses dry out? Do you send a fire hazard warning? And to whom? Somebody has to get equipment in there and cut fire breaks in the tall dry grasses... otherwise."

"The Yerba Buena Fire Department—"

"—Exactly."

"On that question," she advised, "you'll have to ask the fire department. As to the taxes, I think they're paid by the club that holds those summer campouts in the old-growth redwood forests there. After all, they pay a fee to the police department for protection during those summer outings of theirs—to keep the women and protesters at bay."

"What club is that?" Roger pressed, leaning closer to her.

Rosylyn leaned across the counter, and while Roger was admiring her turquoise and silver amulet, she whispered, "The Bavarian Club."

CHAPTER TEN:
DATING ROSYLYN

On their first date that weekend, over drinks at a popular German bistro, Roger asked Rosylyn how he might make contact with the person in charge of the Bavarian Club.

Rosylyn was quick to reply, "My friend Anna will know. We were undergraduates together at Berkeley. She and her husband have just launched their law office. She wrote down Anna's name and her address. "They're specializing in community issues, and that will include the homeless."

"You homeless?" And Roger laughed.

"I live in an SRO, but for showers I have to go to either the YWCA or my friend Grace—she's got a studio apartment—lucky girl." Rosylyn wrote Anna's address and phone number from memory. "She's going to handle my case—I'm supposed to get some support from the Region for housing, but so far they haven't come through. By the way, you homeless?"

Roger shook his head. "Not yet. But my landlord has just raised my rent—no rent control—and unless I can close some deals, I'll soon be out on the streets. I mean, my nest egg from Idaho has gone pretty fast, given the cost of housing and everything else here."

*   *   *

Roger looked up Anna's law firm address on the Internet, telephoned for an appointment—free consultation, as Anna told him it would be—and went to see her. He rode the elevator to the seventh floor, as directed by the building's greeter. As the elevator doors slid aside, a view out over Yerba Buena greeted him when he looked through a glass walled conference room where a large number of very young people were working at computer terminals. A receptionist looked up and asked for his name, and then announced to Anna through a voice connection of some sort, "An older man out here to see you." Startled, Roger thought, well, yes, he had to acknowledge to himself, he was older than those most of the people gathered around the conference table.

Soon Anna came out and they shook hands. "Private Conference Room, Kyra," she instructed the receptionist, who nodded, jotting the time of their occupancy on what looked to Roger like a formal time sheet controlling the room's occupancy. "Please pardon Kyra. She's quite young and still thinks anyone past 30 is old."

After introducing himself, Anna asked what he wanted to talk about. He said, "I'm researching a very large piece of undeveloped land here in Yerba Buena, and I want to contact the owner."

"You want to get a brokerage listing?"

Impressed with Anna's knowledge of the business, Roger nodded, adding the word "exclusive."

"Yes, Mr. Roadhouse, I do know the parcel—quite big—but I haven't looked into how title is held. If you want to engage our legal services, I can do this for you."

"What are your fees, may I ask?"

"You may, and our firm—there are two of us, my husband and me—our fee is two hundred dollars an hour."

"How many hours?"

"Don't really know. Two, at least, I should think, as I suspect the ownership is opaque. So, maybe more."

Roger was unsure what to say.

Anna broke the silence, "I must disclose a possible conflict of interest to you right up front."

"And that is?"

"The ownership, however it may be legally constituted, is a private club, a historic club, of which my father is a director. That much I can tell you for free right here now today. So, if you do engage us, you'll have to decide if you are getting fair legal representation."

Roger said, "Well, just to find facts doesn't create a conflict of interest, I shouldn't think."

"Okay, so far" Anna said. "However, if the ownership is really opaque—such as an offshore trust, or something of that complexity, we may have to engage an attorney who specializes in tax haven jurisdictions."

"But if we're not going to court…"

"Right. For what reason would you file a lawsuit?"

"Don't know at this point. I'm just beginning to explore the situation."

"And so are others," Anna said. "Without betraying any confidences, just by listening at our local bistro, I can tell you this parcel is the subject of a lot of informal conversations."

"Realtors?"

"Some, and lawyers, as well. And the homeless."

"Trouble is," Roger said, "I'm just a real estate broker. I have some homes in escrow, but they don't always close—contingencies, etc." I'm running out of my nest egg that I put together before I left Idaho."

"You homeless?"

"Not yet," and he laughed in embarrassment.

"Tell you what," Anna said, "We'll look into ownership—two hours max of our time. You pay that, and then if we go further into the matter, we'll do it on a contingency basis."

"How would that work?"

Anna looked at Roger intently as she explained, "Our firm will take 20 per cent of any and all brokerage commissions you as a broker get from the sale of all or any portion of the property,"

Roger said, "Then you must think the parcel offers potential? I mean, for making money?"

"Yes, Big money. That is, if someone smart like you can get in the driver's seat." Anna smiled and held up her index finger as she said, "For our society here in Yerba Buena that huge parcel of undeveloped land offers us a solution, that is, a place to build a lot of affordable houses—tiny or even larger—for people who are now living on the streets. Developing that land into housing will be a major step toward solving the homeless problem in Yerba Buena."

* * *

Leaving the communal office building, Roger marveled at how productive their conversation had proven to be, from the point of view of his having made inquiry and learning more about the property, at least what someone else, who was knowledgeable, thought about the potential for the land from a real estate brokerage point of view. Yet wasn't Anna too quick to jump at the opportunity?

He recalled the number of other brokers who had made inquiry with Rosylyn at the local planning department office. Anna was quite eager to ride tandem on his back for her firm's legal fees that she and her husband might eventually derive from his brokerage efforts. Yet those events, if they ever did take place, were off in the future—likely the distant future.

Roger thought about the amount of time and work that could lie ahead for him and the patience required for him to score commissions. He thought about a baseball metaphor: the days, months, and even years of training. There was so much time necessary to even get up to bat. Especially in view of how many players wanted to secure a place on the roster of those trying to score off this piece of land. Quite obviously, he concluded, the game on the field—the Yerba Buena real estate field—was a popular one. It was indeed well attended. Moreover, there appeared to be a lot of additional curious fans watching from the stands, not just the bleachers, but the press box, and the private luxury condominium boxes overlooking the field, as well. Were all competition? Maybe not all, but likely most. Swarming to make money off the big parcel, money going in, and money coming out. A good broker gets both directions from off one piece of land.

CHAPTER ELEVEN:
THE BIG PLAYER IN TOWN

L ater that evening, out in front of his modest apartment building, Roger was obviously pleading with a woman, yet his gesticulations seemed to be getting him nowhere, nor his words either. "In Boise, Mrs. Dante, no one would dare do this to anyone," he said. "We're kind to one another. We're nice—"

"—Then go back to Boise, Mr. a... ah..." Slowly she smiled a sinister smile and added, "Tomorrow noon, and that's it. I'm being more than generous given the tight housing picture here in Yerba Buena."

Roger thought he could get something for his car, but what does a realtor do without a car? In what he thought would be his most persuasive voice, he tried, "I'm on the verge of getting a listing, a big listing, Mrs. Dante, plus two of my single family house brokerage deals are in escrow. They are prominent executive buyers with money to close."

"Borrow from the escrow," she said in a sarcastic tone, as if one could to that, but of course one couldn't and she knew it. And so did Roger. "Three people want your apartment, any one of which will pay half again what your rent is." She turned away, likely to disappear back into her apartment building like a tortoise retreating into its protective shell.

Then, as if from nowhere, Roger thought he heard his name being called. He turned to see a chauffeur-driven limousine pull up to the curb next to him. From the opening window, a head with penetrating blue eyes and flowing blonde hair peered at him. Fingers on her hand, bejeweled with several rings, grasped the open window's ledge. As she spoke, her necklace adorned with fascinating jewels sparkled in the evening sun. But it was the smile with her perfect teeth, her alluring lipstick—where'd she get that beguiling tone—he wondered as he forgot about his landlady who had left him standing at the curb.

"Mr. Roadhouse," the voice from the limo repeated his name as the door opened and Miss Milan Runway in Yerba Buena made her fashionable appearance. No, he thought, it was Miss Business Woman of the Year, or if not, she should be so captioned, for she was dressed the part. He visualized her portrait on, well, Fortune, or Business Week, or no, more likely on the center gallery in the Art Museum of Important Women on the Planet.

Roger realized, of course, response was his to do, but before he could take his eyes off her stunning personal appearance and formulate his set of appropriate words, she decreed in an affirmative feminine voice, "I want you to work for me, Mr. Roadhouse. Starting right now." Not pausing for his answer, she demanded to know, "What do you say?"

Roger remained speechless while noticing she was now calling after his landlady and taking out a bundle of bills from her designer purse. "How much, Mrs.?"

The landlady, too, was suddenly speechless and could only nod and extend her hand when the visitor offered the bills to her. She managed, "Two Thousand for now." Ms. Fashion Statement waited only a millisecond before requiring, "I'll need a receipt for one month's rent." The landlady produced her receipt book and wrote in the number along with Roger's name and unit number, then performed a sort of curtsy and mumbled what Roger thought was, "Thank you, Ms. Marmon."

"Get in!" Ms. Stylish commanded, and Roger did, first holding the door for her before going around the car and getting in on the other side. "Where'd you learn to do that?" Ms. Vogue asked.

"Do what?"

"Treat women with respect."

"You just did me, and I just did you."

"Respect."

Roger nodded.

"You're a good broker."

"And you?"

"The best. In Yerba Buena." And she gestured at her chauffeur and car as her collection of jewelry flashed again.

"And I work for myself," he said, trying to establish what he though might turn into a negotiating stance.

"You're from Boise." A statement.

"You know that? Yes, I have been here a short time."

"I know. And I know about how clever you were in unloading those new houses by the Boise airport runway."

"So, what is? I mean, your name." By now they were driving near the ocean. The houses were large, very large. The car idled in front of one while the chauffeur activated a beam, causing the garage door to rise. The car drove somewhat downward into an underground garage, parking next to a vintage motorcar.

"Marmon," she said, pointing to it. "Think of the luxury Marmon Sixteen automobile as you trace your fingers delicately along the leather and wood trim."

Roger looked again at her, his eyes lingering here and there. She was even more elegant in the subdued lighting of her underground garage than in the natural evening sunlight. He watched her reflection in the polished black of the vintage Marmon motorcar. "In Boise we're not in the Yerba Buena loop, so I don't know about your firm, or even your name."

She reached into her purse and handed him a business card and waited a quick few seconds while he studied it. "The commission split for you will be 70-30. The seventy per cent is for you, of course."

"30 for you." Roger waited. "Right now the split for me is 100. Period."

"Might as well make it 1000 because you'll never get the deal."

"Why's that?" But as he asked, he saw she was moving lithely out of the car without his holding the door open for her. Promptly she floated toward an exit door of the underground garage without an invitation for to him to follow. Was she going to leave him here in her garage? Alone? For the night? What's with this woman? "Wait," he said, but she kept moving. She's a master negotiator, he thought, better tuned to the art than he for sure, he acknowledged, uncertainty ruling his emotions.

He got out of the car. Before she opened the garage's interior door, she pointed to what looked like an embedded microphone adjacent to the door, as the chauffeur preceded her through the door offering a mini-salute to her as she said to Roger, "Here's an intercom. Push the red button if you want to come in and talk more to me; otherwise there's a onc-way exit door to the street." She gestured behind him. "Buses run every 30 minutes, till 2 AM." The garage door closed, and the lights went out.

Roger groped for the red button on the intercom next to the door, finally seeing its faint glimmer. He stood motionless in the dark next to the button, its dull red now beaming back at him. Then he saw a medley of red reflections from off the Marmon's chrome mirrors and polished automotive skin as dull red played a cacophony of directional signals, along with the various reds from a second vintage motor car next to it, one he had thought was a Packard, but had not taken time, nor was he that interested, to search for a nameplate on its hood or grill.

A long moment of silence, his moment of self-induced indecisive silence. Standing in the dark, in the garage, in the quiet, in what was becoming a forced focus on his dilemma at hand, Roger gradually sought the structure of his situation: Apparently he had immersed himself in a unique drama having to do with a parcel of land, its use, its ownership, its potential development, coupled with an amount of money that might be made off its brokerage and, in addition, even its development. That is, assuming the right scenario for its listing and its development could be choreographed. For her? For Him?

Roger began to realize the stakes were high. Ms. Milan Runway, likely one of the most effective real estate brokers in Yerba Buena, was playing a high stakes game, as well, and he had likely stumbled into an unusual role in her deck of cards that she wanted played on her table, perhaps an inside straight in which she needed him. Why else her offer? Why else her paying his apartment rent?

If he were to exit the garage and leave in the bus, he would be effectively exiting the game at hand, folding his cards, and choosing a path that would run contrary to Ms. Milan Runway, that is, Ms. Marmon, and her scheming mind. So, where did she fit into this land parcel's picture and how? And where could he fit?

It was time he found out if his wits and negotiating skills were equal to hers? Probably not, he concluded, warning himself against yielding to her challenge by pushing the dim red button.

CHAPTER TWELVE:
THE SENSE WITHIN

Most places, Roger had always thought, most towns, certainly little villages, even large towns (maybe not so much in these days of megalomanias) emit the feelings of a sense of place. In Boise, he had felt that sense of place. Boise was a place, a town, a city, a feeling. It had its edges, its limits, beyond which you were out in rural Idaho. This same feeling of place was true in other towns in Idaho and in Eastern Oregon. Yet today in the category of so many megalopolises, there was not much left of such feelings, so Roger lamented. Oh, Yerba Buena had its docks, its parks, its high rises, its old Spanish Mission, its history, going back to Spain and Mexico, and, yes, up north, once briefly to Russia, but today was there a lingering sense of place, a sense of spirit, a sense of boundaries, the limits, the city limits, that point beyond where eventually you were somewhere else? Probably not, he concluded. Yerba Buena seemed to go on forever. Of course, he realized, everything, every place, had its limits.

Yet Yerba Buena was one big, almost endless megalopolis, swarming with people, jobs, companies, overloaded with retail stores, packed with used car lots, with new car lots, strings of big box stores, cobwebby freeways, crowded mass transit, noises from all directions, as the commotion of civilization forged its cacophony. Where was quiet, silence, peace? Everything was coming at you. Day was night and night was day. Holidays were workdays and workdays were holidays. You weren't good enough, skilled enough, educated enough, smart enough, savvy enough. You were lacking the skills to just get by, or if you had those, not the cleverness to get ahead, to score, to make it big, to become important. But why, Roger now asked himself, did he want to do that—why did he want to make a lot of money and show the world he was clever, more clever than most guys or gals his age?

Maybe he just wanted to go back to when he was a carpenter helping his father build houses in Boise. Maybe he just wanted to craft an arch in a house, frame a living room, build kitchen cabinets, stand back and admire his work and go home at night and be proud he had created something tangible. For Yerba Buena, as he was coming to feel and sense, was not a tangible place, but instead a hubbub, an indescribable event unfolding day after day like a giant aberrant amoeba out of control. No one knew where it was going, or why, it was just expanding like a balloon, a never-ending balloon that wasn't going to run out of air or shell, and wasn't going to burst, either. A dirigible that some day would be bigger than the heavens it was supposed to navigate.

So, why should he push the tiny red button? Ms. Fashion? Ms. Vogue? Ms. Best Real Estate Broker west of the Pecos. Why? Because she was smarter than he, or better connected, or more aggressive, or... and he wanted to find out what force, what carrot, what enticement drove her, just as much as he wanted to find out what drove Yerba Buena. And what was driving himself... as he pushed the red button.

CHAPTER THIRTEEN:
ALLEN'S ARTICLE

Angelika read Allen White's feature article in his nationwide magazine, a copy of which he FedExed to her days before it appeared online or hit the remaining Yerba Buena newsstands.

Rosylyn read Allen's article in the magazine, which she'd bought at her favorite bookstore.

Roger read the article when Rosylyn gave him her copy and told him to read it.

"Goody" read Allen's article immediately after Mario had asked him about it. He'd gone to the reading room, grabbed the club's copy and sat in the nearest leather wingback chair after ordering a scotch, beginning to read.

Anna went to the closest library and persuaded the librarian to let her read the copy before it was put on the display shelf.

Most bookstores and newsstands still left around Yerba Buena had pretty well sold out their copies by evening.

Elsewhere, John Riley, head of the small organization of descendants of the Patricios, in his home in Phoenix, also read Allen White's article.

CHAPTER FOURTEEN:
MS. INTRIGUE

The door opened. He entered... slowly... not knowing what to expect, what he would see, and would she be there, waiting, with a conquering smile on her subtly made-up face?

He heard water. Splashing. And music. Soft classical music. The lighting was dim, subdued, soft, not glaring like a retail shopping district, but more like a monastery, not that he'd ever been in one, but what he imagined it to be. And was he on the path to become a practicing monk in the following of this real estate guru, this Ms. Milan Runway?

Then there she was, all of sudden, as if out of a fog of the unknown, stark naked, except, except, and he was almost afraid, for he spotted an American Army pistol in a holster attached to her jeweled belt, its gems glistening. People in Boise had bodies, of course, but none like hers.

"Why the pistol?" was all he could manage.

"A backup to my two dogs, Ayn and Rand." Her long bronze hair swished in the direction of where he now saw two Afghan hounds. Chained to long leashes. "Chiparus," she told him, the Romanian/French bronze sculptor of strong women a hundred years ago. And there were strong women back then."

"As now," he said, his eyes darting from the dogs to the pistol to the rest of her, not knowing in his fright where to linger. Then in a visual sweep, he saw the bronze sculpture on a table: two Afghans, a shapely young women, holding onto their leashes as the hounds seemed to be pulling her through life.

"You see, if you were an intruder, I'd be in charge." The dogs eyed him with suspicion. "You'd be toast."

"But I'm not... toast, that is."

"Let's get down to business, Mr. Boise, Idaho." And she pulled a Tibetan robe from a bronze hook, slipped it over her body and pointed to a door, through which she lithely moved, he following. She sat in a vintage Sheraton chair at a small feminine Sheraton desk, motioning for him to occupy a Herman Miller chair in front.

She picked up a brass Tibetan bell and rang it once. A person attired in a monk's dark red robe entered and asked, "Tea?"

"Two."

"We'll have five minutes of silence," she said as she struck a different bell, this one brass, the sound waves reverberating around the room, then again, and once more. Then silence.

Roger started to speak, but ten seductive red fingernails signaled him to stop. "First, let's settle in," she decreed. "We will follow our breathing, you and me, then move on."

*   *   *

He did as told, and was glad to do so. Settling in, Roger's mind went blank, albeit briefly, then it began to wander, to speculate, to imagine. Soon, with each in and out breath, he felt his mind tingling in anticipation, the bell's musical vibrations growing into an entrancing tintinnabulation.

CHAPTER FIFTEEN:
501.C3

"Your contributions are tax deductible," "Goody," declared as he struggled to straighten his tux's errant bow tie. "Have to wear the damn things at these fund-raising events," he mumbled to himself. And then with verbal force he repeated his tax saving message into the hand-held microphone. He moved among the Bavarian Club's dinner guests, adding, "Each of you can help the homeless and save on your income taxes, federal and state, and you can do it all with one signature on one check. My friends, it's time for all of us to climb aboard our club's charity to help the homeless. I urge you as civic-minded citizens to do so."

Many applauded. It was a gender mix evening, one of the rare events when women were allowed inside the Bavarian Club. They were mostly couples, mostly but not all married. "Goody's" unmarried couplette had applauded his statement the loudest, Chief Steward Mario thought as he watched the proceedings, alert to retrieve any fresh orders for a patron's drink.

Ready to yank off the bow tie and cast it onto the carpeted floor, "Goody" grimaced as it suddenly popped around in front of his mouth, stifling his attempt at mentioning the charity's 501.c3 status. Thwarted from delivering the next repetition of his tax and homeless saving message, he lamented his embarrassment. Seeing his angst, Mario started toward "Goody" to help correct the tie's behavior, but "Goody's" female companion jumped up and was standing by his side before Mario could get there. He heard "Goody" whisper, "Thanks, Emm!"

"Tell them about the charity, 'Goody,'" Mario overheard the woman called Emm instruct him, "You know, I am the only woman on the charity's board." Mario saw him nod as Emm maneuvered into her chair as she acknowledged the polite nods and smiles of those at their table. Mario had seen the woman before in the club.

67

Once, he had picked up a nametag that had slipped off her dress. Before he handed it back to her, he couldn't help but read her name, "Ms. Marmon."

Tie straightened with her help, "Goody" went on, "Let me enlighten you all here this evening as to our charity's plan for the homeless. Homes for Everyone—the name of our 501.c3 non-profit—has taken over the abandoned Barnes and Noble Bookstore two blocks up the street and is planning to install cubicles for the homeless. Roger Authoright, our H for E chairman, tells me they can get at least 50 tiny areas in there, that is, if they can raise the money for the refurbishing and also paying the Region's hefty application fees. That's where you all come in."

"Whiskers" grimaced. His cleric collar bulged as he swallowed hard, then again, this time with a magnified martini (very dry) gulp. He turned to his attorney, whose wife also happened to be sitting with the holy man and Mrs. Whiskers. "Guy, you've got to stop them. I'll be damned if I'm going to give to this cause—have all those homeless beggars across the street from our condominium building. I'm on the Board there, and I know my fellow board members, not to mention each and every resident will be opposed to this scheme."

Guy's eyebrows rose. He sad, "We'll file for an extended Environmental Impact Report—that'll stop 'em for six months while we prepare our lawsuit. They must be in violation of some zoning regulation—converting a former bookstore into a homeless hangout." The attorney added, "By that time all these pledges "Flowers" there is getting this evening will have expired, and the project will never go trough. Meanwhile, the building owners will be compelled to convert the old bookstore into a half dozen or so luxury condominiums."

"Whiskers" sighed a relief emotion, and then waved off "Flowers" with his iPad and request for a donation to the cause. "Wrong cause," he muttered, adding, "misguided" to the automatic nod of Mrs. Whiskers.

"Flowers" was attired in the latest of tuxedo designs." He was circulating from one table to the next, complimenting a select few of the women present on their designer dresses, his main mission being to record the names and amounts of those making pledges. In the process he made out a receipt that he handed to each donor, having entered the information into a file on his iPad.

The Bavarian Club dining hall was full to capacity with club members and invited guests from the business and social establishment of Yerba Buena. Hurrying in to grab the two remaining seats reserved for them were Angelika and husband Peter.

"Goody" maneuvered over to them to shake her hand and perfunctorily acknowledge her husband. "Thanks for joining us this evening," he offered.

"It's a good cause," Angelika said to "Goody" as Mario brought them the introductory champagne glasses. She sipped and quipped to the host, "Your charity's plan, while meritorious, is only a drop in the bucket for our homeless." She paused, allowing her remark to register, and then added, "Of course, 'Goody,' you know that."

"Goody" grunted an affirmation, philosophizing, "Got to start somewhere."

In a marriage so time-consumed with respective business and social responsibilities, and packed with meetings, memos, and mundane lists there was precious little time to allow time to share with one's spouse much information about their respective days. This evening's social dinner was no exception. So, Angelika felt obliged to inform her husband Peter in a discreet whisper, "This private club is sitting on the largest piece of undeveloped real estate anywhere in or within commuting distance of Yerba Buena."

Peter thought for a moment, downed his champagne with a quick tilt of the glass, and queried, "Angie, do you realize how much power your quasi-government agency wields?"

"Why do you say that?" She asked.

Peter smiled knowingly and wrote with his designer pen on the linen tablecloth the two words, "Eminent Domain."

CHAPTER SIXTEEN:
EMINENT DOMAIN

Earlier that afternoon, attorney Anna and husband Jeremy, with their client Roger, were documenting the ownership of this same extensive parcel of land.

Anna said, "Here's what we've found. You've probably gotten this same information from Rosylyn at the Region's local property office." Anna recited the name of the partnership and legal address, as listed in Bahamas records in Nassau.

Roger pressed, "In a practical sense, what does that mean? Who can I go to and see about getting a broker's listing?"

Anna referred to her notes. "Our legal correspondent in Nassau has told us the minimum amount of public information available, namely the dummy name and the post office box address in Nassau, the rest hidden under the laws of that Caribbean country. Of course, the actual owner is indeed here in Yerba Buena. Anna smiled. "I suspected the answer, but I wanted to be certain before reporting to you."

Roger waited in anticipation.

Anna disclosed, "It is my father's private club. Well, not really his alone, for he's acting in the capacity as the chairman of the Board of the private Bavarian Club."

Roger smiled, "And I'm not to reveal that I am your client."

"Exactly."

Roger mused and then asked, "What are the odds they want to sell?"

Anna said, "Next to nil."

"So, is it a dead end. I mean, getting a listing."

Jeremy said, "There are ways. That is why we're interested in being part of your effort, given this historic time of runaway homelessness here in Yerba Buena."

Roger pressed, "So, what is my... our... next move?"

Anna advised, "As your legal counsel, I am telling you that, in our considered opinion, your next move is to pursue the legal concept of eminent domain."

Jeremy asked, "Do you know what that is? How it works?"

"Yes," Roger replied. "It's on most state brokerage examinations, so I'm aware of the concept. It's based on public need, public good. But we can't initiate it here, can we? We're not a government. We can't just wave a wand in the newspaper's legal ads column and announce to the world that we're taking over their land for the public benefit."

"Of course not. But I know who may have the power to do so."

Roger whistled. He stared at Anna. "What are you saying? How could I... we... fit into the picture?"

"You're a licensed real estate broker in this state. Your task is to figure out how." Sternly, Jeremy reminded, "Remember, Roger, we have a client-lawyer agreement."

"Of course," Roger said in a matter of fact tone. In a stronger voice, he questioned, "But, explain to me: isn't government the only entity that can go to court and try to exercise such power?"

Anna commented, "Yes, usually, but not always. Let me share with you some of the material in my law school thesis about who can press the matter of eminent domain. I'll base my summary on court cases." She opened a thick notebook that Roger saw was labeled "Eminent Domain." From it, she pulled out a bound paper report with her name at the top. He saw it was graded A+. Refreshing her memory, she spoke further:

"Let's start with the 5th Amendment to the U.S. Constitution. It gives the government the power to take private property for public use and benefit so long as there is just compensation to the landowner."

She continued, "Now we get into the uses that justify government take-over lawsuits. They fall under the category of public benefit projects, such as highways, airports, even professional athletic stadiums. The list of such uses is fairly long and includes urban renewal projects."

Roger fidgeted. "Our Constitution was written more than 200 years ago. Where do things stand today?"

Jeremy said, "There's a recent Supreme Court decision."

"5 to 4," Anna said. "It surprised a lot of legal scholars and real estate developers, as well. The city of New London, Connecticut prevailed. The court ruled that it was for the benefit of the people of the city."

"What was the project?" Roger asked.

"To build a new pharmaceutical factory. The court allowed the taking by the developer of several pieces of private property."

"How did they justify that?"

"Because it was purportedly for the public good."

"Based on what?"

"The City argued that they were accomplishing a number of things for the public benefit; namely, providing jobs to the people who would be building the factory plus those who would work in it. Also, the city argued they were eliminating the blight that existed in several of the parcels—trash, rodents, that sort of disease-causing blight. In other words, everyone in and around New London would be a winner. Of course, the private land owners were compensated."

"Of course."

"And I suppose fairly."

Anna nodded and went on, "The concept, Roger, is that property owners are giving up some or all of their property for the benefit of the common interest, that is, the greater interest of the city, of society, of civilization… if you will." And each time in the process compensating the sellers with something of value. That's typically money—coin of the realm. But let us pose the question as to what constitutes value."

Roger exclaimed, "Got it."

"Do you see where we're going?"

"Absolutely!" Roger said. He beamed at the attorneys. But then he grew silent, thoughtful, and was soon looking frustrated. "But in our situation what government is involved, or what developer? Who are the players? You know, I need to think this through."

Anna nodded, "So do we, but here's where we are advising you to play the first eminent domain card." She paused and reminisced, "In my college days, I came to befriend a woman on the law school faculty who had the reputation of being brilliant. Today she holds one of the most powerful positions in Yerba Buena as head of the Regional governmental authority." Anna waited, and getting no indication one way or the other from Roger, made her suggestion. As your attorney representing you, I can call her and make an appointment for the three of us to meet with her."

"That's fine," Roger readily agreed, then asked, "But what will be our conversational goal?"

"First off, after we present her with our idea, I suspect she'll remonstrate, citing what we call the "taking clause" of the Fifth Amendment. In other words, she'll react by saying her agency could never raise the necessary billions of dollars needed to compensate the land owners in this case even if her agency were to successfully pursue the idea of eminent domain. She will tell us, so I anticipate, that it would take a monstrous municipal bond issue that, first off, would never be approved by the voters throughout the Region. She might underscore that by saying that, even if approved by voters—the odds of about zero, given voters' reluctance to pass bond issues—the bond would never be underwritten by a Wall Street investment banking firm. In other words, there'll be no real money forthcoming to implement the idea, so your idea is as dead as a dodo bird from the get-go. She'll balk right there."

Roger scoffed, "So, it'll be a waste of our time, including my fee to you guys, and a waste of her time, as well."

Anna smiled. "That's where you, in your societal brilliance, come in."

"Me?"

"Think about it, Roger... what arguments could you come up with to dissuade her from closing it off right there and then?" Anna paused and acknowledged, "However, I'm beginning to formulate a train of thought—an argument, that is."

In the ensuing silence, Roger felt he should disclose to them, "I met this real estate woman..."

"And?"

"She wants me to work for her."

"Doing what?"

"Brokerage, of course."

"We have an agreement with you," Jeremy reminded.

Roger nodded his understanding, adding, "But you must know that she is most persuasive and most talented." He visualized her figure, heard her voice, marveled at her fashion statement, and saw again the sparkle in her jewelry. All the while, he struggled to place in their appropriate squares the various chess pieces looking up at him from the checkered real estate board. Yet Roger came up short as to his relationship with this Ms. Marmon. Prodding himself onward, he visualized bags of gold coin, while admitting to himself that these monetary rewards were way off in the distance.

"Who is she?" Anna interrupted his dreamlike state, her voice growing insistent.

Roger sensed he was working his way into a box, or rather a thick huge paper bag, where punching his way out was going to border on the impossible. For a moment he felt as if he were back in Boise, standing in the winter chill staring hopelessly at his father's inventory of unsold homes. He shivered in the cold Boise wind without the comforting warmth of a sales solution. He worried he was frozen in place without being able to ignite his way out?

Anna repeated her demand, her voice firm. Jeremy rising from his chair, loomed over Roger, demanding, "Who is this woman?"

Trying to formulate some sort of an explanation, Roger hesitated before telling them, "She is Ms. Marmon."

"Oh," Anna said. "I bet she covets part of your commission… if not most of it."

"That's how she makes money, and it appears to me she's made a lot of it."

Anna decreed, "But we'll head her off, for we're going to get— that is you, as a broker, are going to get the exclusive listing on this parcel of land because your position will be verified and certified by the court."

Jeremy said, "That is, if we have a legal say in the matter."

"Which we will," Anna proclaimed.

"How can you be so certain?" Roger pressed.

Quickly, Jeremy's precise words, spoken slowly and powerfully, followed in answer, "Roger, allow me to tell you why I went to law school and, now having passed the Bar, am pursuing my unique legal career."

"Please," Roger said with some relief from his nascent fumbling explanation about Ms. Milan Runway. Smiling he said, "I need inspiration."

"Anna can speak for herself, but as for me, let me begin by describing for you how my take on the law and those who practice it has evolved."

Anna looked at her husband, her brown eyes sparkling, encouraging.

Jeremy sat down and, looking squarely at Roger, began: "All my life, through school, through debating societies, through legal conferences, through Buddhist retreats, through meditation and mediations, I have harnessed my creative energy to asses the legal profession and the laws that govern us."

Roger thought about the daunting challenges that had confronted him in Boise real estate and how his thoughtful take on the profession had developed through his own observations. He said, "I'd like to hear your story."

Jeremy said, "I came from a very poor family. My father was unemployed a good portion of his life; attorneys and debt collectors hounded us. My mother took in seamstress work to help make ends meet. I began to work in high school and then applied for and got a scholarship to a small law school, finally transferring to Boalt where I met Anna."

"We were in the same class on foreclosures."

"The cases we studied and the discussions that ensued caused me to begin to form my own comparisons between the moral and ethical values on one side of life versus the established rule of law on the other. Since that time I have been formulating my own views, pursuing a dedicated mission of contrasting the two."

"Go on," Roger urged.

"You see, Roger, the law in our country is made up of codified law, that is, it is written by elected representatives, legal scholars, and government staffers through their writing of the regulations, for example."

Roger nodded, "Law books by the shelf in law libraries."

Jeremy went on, "In our court system, interpretations of the law are subject to judges' whims and biases. Oh, maybe there's the odd grand jury or regular jury, but it's mostly up to the judges, case judges, appellate judges, supreme-over-the-other-judges."

"Seems an accurate and familiar description," Roger allowed.

"That axiom ties us to the past, often to the distant past. Attorneys must research the past and cite past laws and yesterday's court decisions as they prepare today's arguments. Judges rely on past court decisions, that is, their interpretations of those decisions. As a result, in the courts, as well as in our lives, we are each of us forced to live in the past. The past is our teacher and gives us guidance, whether or not it is appropriate for today's world."

Anna added, "Many beliefs are based on the past—events, teachings, requiring us to bow to concepts coming to us from the distant past. Society, meanwhile, is moving forward along new and exploratory pathways. Many people are thinking differently, behaving differently, talking differently, texting to each other, to many in a strange new dialect, yet understanding each other. As a result, nothing and no one stays the same. Impermanence rules our lives but not so in the law."

Jeremy smiled and said emphatically, "I have vowed to update the past, bring us into the 21st century by taking steps to reform the law."

"How will you possibly do that?" Roger asked.

Jeremy smiled. "With your help, Roger. With the situation now facing us, we are going to begin to make changes. You see, I have conceived new ideas for applying the law. New techniques to advance it, to improve its dialogue, to make it more meaningful to each and every member of the general public. I want to try to apply the new law to every citizen. I yearn to redesign our legal fabric. However, most often the warp and the weft are stiff in their intransigence, like a frozen and inoperative loom. The status quo confronts new ideas, wanting to ward off all attempts at change. The result is that the fabric on which we are working remains fixed in place with the shuttlecock stuck in immobility."

"Laudatory thinking," Roger complimented.

Anna voiced, "I'm a fighting member of Jeremy's crusade."

Wanting to know, admiration in his voice, Roger pressed, "What are the embryonic ideas you advocate?"

Jeremy said, "Now, here today with you, we have our opportunity."

Roger waited as Anna explained, "To carry Jeremy's argument further, I want to point out that in order to implement the taking clause, the law specifies just compensation must be paid to the land owners." She stood and paced around the table and addressed Roger, "But what do you think constitutes just compensation?"

"Money."

"Of course." Anna sat down, looked at her husband, and instructed, "Tell him what else, Counselor."

Now, it was Jeremy's turn to pace, as his thoughts were being formulated in prep for his summary. Speaking deliberately, choosing his words carefully, so Roger thought, Jeremy began to describe his concept of compensation: "Compensation can take many forms, colors, and shapes. As you just said, we automatically think of money, coin of the realm, gold bars, cashier's checks, automatic wire bank deposits, and so forth. But, I ask you, look at corporate America, our government, all the many non-profits and consider how they compensate their executives."

Anna injected, "There are many ways that do not always deliver money right now. For example, think about pensions, health coverage for executives and their families. Corporate executives also benefit from social contacts in their country clubs, free legal advice from in-house attorneys when they need it. They get recognition through memberships in exclusive social clubs and organizations, all of which are theirs for no money."

Roger urged, "But back to our situation at hand."

Jeremy nodded, "So here's how we're going to compensate the owners of this monstrous private club in our eminent domain lawsuit: Think first of what this huge parcel in the middle of Yerba Buena might be worth in monetary terms."

Roger said, "Priceless. I mean priceless. It might take years and never-ending legal fees, lawsuits, appraisal fees, and heaven knows what other expenses, let alone the passage of time to arrive at a fair value in money terms. Even then there would likely follow more lawsuits appealing the decision."

"Exactly. In order to meet the requirement of the Fifth Amendment 'taking clause,'" Anna said.

Jeremy continued to pace and describe his view of the taking clause: "The owners—or rather the entity that owns this huge parcel—is controlled by an exclusive group of the wealthiest men in Yerba Buena. In fact, I know from researching the membership, that you must have a FICO score above 800 to be considered for membership. In addition, your net worth must be approaching one billion dollars, and you must be a college graduate with at least two degrees. Moreover, your home address must be within socially approved neighborhoods."

"You may have thought we got rid of mortgage lending discrimination in the old days, which was labeled as red-lining?" Anna asked. "Think again, for now the same racial and ethnic bias shows up in how lenders view our FICO scores."

Jeremy laughed, "Like I'd never qualify for any sort of credit with my bottom basement score. Serious again, he added, "Also, for membership in the Bavarian Club you must be recommended by at least five members. I mean, who among us ordinary folks can qualify for membership in their club? It's only a few of the very wealthy, the very well connected, the very—yes, and I'll use the select term—Important People—the V.I.P.s who are authorized to play in their private league."

Roger said, "That list is limited to maybe a half of one percent of the population."

"Exactly," Jeremy echoed.

Roger stood and also began to pace. "So, you're saying that today these men and their wives don't need money; they've got tons of it already. They enjoy top-of-the-hill social prestige. In short, they've got everything you, when you were a little boy or girl, dreamt of getting in your future adult life."

Anna asked, "So, think what it is that they do need. What additional perks could they yearn for?"

Jeremy stopped pacing. As did Roger. He looked at Jeremy who answered, "What they must have, for themselves, for their families, and for their grandchildren, is the safety of their property, assurances that their personal and family prestige is honored and will continue to be preserved—that their status in society is cast in stone for ever and ever."

Roger added, "Safety in their stability. But maybe they don't realize what they actually want. We've got to explain it to them, remind them of their vulnerability to change, to being threatened with violence from the masses if they don't...."

Anna added, "As well as tell the court our plan to save their security—that's the payment that will compensate them."

Roger said, "That is, when and if we get to the court trial."

Jeremy pronounced with assurance, "We'll get there. Trust me!"

"Tell me again, what is your argument to get us there?" Roger asked him.

Jeremy summed up his argument, "Here's my take: Their answer and our answer is that they want to know their way of life is not going to be threatened. It will not be challenged by the people they call riff-raff who are rioting in the streets, threatening to invade their homes, steal their precious property and overthrow the government they control. In their established power realm, these wealthy men in the Bavarian Club fear the people. They fear the lesser people who, in their biased judgment, are going to rise up, take control and force them to change their system into some strange unknown and fearful system in which one morning they will wake up and find themselves wandering helplessly on the same playing field as the homeless roaming the streets. They want assurances that there are no threats to the ideals they cherish or to their very lives. They want to know their values and their property will endure."

Anna said, "We must explain our argument to the court in terms the judge will understand."

"And that will be when?" Roger puzzled.

Jeremy beamed. "You want to see a homeless genius reveal his theory of homelessness and its relativity to the Yerba Buena universe?"

Roger laughed. Anna beamed. Jeremy explained, "Civilization's benefit. Society's benefit. Those are their benefits. These wealthy men have the most to lose in any sort of major change in society, especially in a revolution. They have the most money, the most property at stake in a social upheaval. What they don't know and don't understand—and what we must explain to them and convince them of—that what is good for the people is good for them and for their stock market investments. That means, in the process, enhancing their personal net worth. You may say that worth is made up only of money, but there are other ingredients in calculating one's valuation of worth. One is self-esteem. For the ultra-wealthy, self-esteem means something irreplaceable in the eyes of the society they dominate. This is unique for their lot. In their value system their worth, their self-esteem, their reputation—all of which must be protected and which will also benefit society, that is the rest of us poor homeless slobs with minus FICO scores, as well. We improve our lot and they advance theirs. It's all for the good of mankind, their mankind and our mankind."

"And womankind," Anna added. "I know all this—all that Jeremy proposes, because I grew up in my father's household of privilege. I know how he and his cohorts think. I know and understand their value judgments."

Roger applauded and said. "You have a sea-changing idea, Jeremy." But his mood quickly changed as he queried, "Is there any legal precedent for your argument?"

"None whatsoever."

The room turned silent.

Anna soon whispered, "We've just heard Jeremy's cutting edge for the legal profession—a bevy of new ideas."

Jeremy added, "Of course, we need a judge who is willing to advance legal precedent into a new realm by adding his own personal evaluation and, for the sake of society, also add his own conviction to the "taking clause" in the concept of eminent domain. Maybe a judge with a low FICO score."

CHAPTER SEVENTEEN:
THE DISEÑO

R oger and Rosylyn met the next evening after her work ended. They were in a bar called "The Mysterious Monkey" that overlooked a stream flowing into the nearby bay.

Their beers having been served, Rosylyn explained, "Rumor is that at midnight in this part of town, along the little stream outside at a full moon, monkeys come out of the underbrush and climb part way up the trunks of the palm trees. From there they howl. But if you listen carefully, so the story goes, you soon discover they're not howling at all but conveying some sort of mysterious message."

"And what is their message?"

"As a worker in the documents department of the local office of the Region, what I hear may not be what other people hear. My mind and hearing are attuned to the chain of title on real estate parcels all over my area of responsibility. So, I see and hear information that has to do with my chosen field." She chuckled. "There, I made a joke. Real estate. Field. You're supposed to laugh."

"Consider that I'm laughing," Roger said, his impatience evident, wanting her to continue as he bottomed-up his brew.

Noting his impatience, Rosylyn proclaimed, "My mother told me, 'Don't beat around the bush.'"

He allowed, "Good advice."

Rosylyn went on, asking, "Have you examined the chain of title on our huge parcel of undeveloped land? I mean, going way back, did you discover who owned the land at the beginning of recorded time, and then who after that, and so forth during the history we in the know call 'chain of title'?"

Roger shook his head. "No, I haven't, but I'm guessing you have. So, please enlighten me. Tell me about this chain of title."

"Diseño," Rosylyn declared, adding with a knowing smile, "You probably never heard the word—Spanish, actually."

"You're probably right." It was Roger's turn to chuckle.

Rosylyn said, "The idea of a chain of title is that if you void or blemish one of the links in the chain, which is the legal history of the title, every event after that suspect link—well, those questionable links in the chain may be thrown into the ownership round file."

"And, so—"

"—And so, that may be what we have here with this desirable gigantic parcel of land. I can't say for sure because I'm not a title insurance officer nor am I an attorney. I'm just a clerk in the land office of the Regional land authority trying to do my job while for fun making out with you."

Roger smiled, but his thoughts were deviating from a desired logical path as he asked, "Do we have a title problem?"

"*May have* are the operative words."

"Who else knows about this possible uncertainty in the title?"

"No one, so far as I know. Just you and me."

Roger thought, ordered another beer and said, "You mentioned the word 'diseño.' What is that?"

"The chain of title on this huge parcel of land begins with the change of ownership that occurred between the Native Americans who owned it—and I use the term loosely—because they had no actual paper document entitling them to what you and I call ownership, that is, the paper or recorded title that we, in our advanced society, hold dear today as evidence of ownership."

Rosylyn wanted another beer. Roger thought about what she was saying and asked, "Okay, so who was the first valid Western or European owner, given our legal definition?"

"Baron Wilhelm von Herzog from Bavaria."

"How did he get the land."

"A Mexican land grant was apparently signed over to him in 1848."

"When Yerba Buena was still part of Mexico?"

Rosylyn nodded, adding, "In the last few days before the treaty took effect."

"So where's the imperfection, if there is one?"

"Diseño."

"Damn it, Rosylyn, who is or what the hell is a 'diseño?'" Roger went to the bar and demanded two more drafts. He asked the bartender if she knew what a diseño was.

"Sure. He comes in here all the time." She laughed, then advised, "You better not have too many of these beers, Mr. a... ah..." The bartender suggested, "Maybe you want to look the word up in my dictionary. To Roger's nod, she turned to her left and called out, "Hey, Henry pass down our dictionary." Henry replied, "I'm still looking up words." She assured him, "I'll give it right back." The book slid down the length of the polished mahogany and Roger grabbed it. Together the bartender and Roger read: "Diseño—a hand-drawn topographical map defining a Mexican land grant."

Roger rushed back to Rosylyn with the definition.

She said, "Yes, but wait, there's more."

"Not in the definition."

"No, but it's what did or didn't happen to the diseño after the treaty of Guadalupe-Hidalgo was signed."

"What was supposed to happen?"

Rosylyn told him about how Congress created the Board of Land Commissioners, telling him that from a chain of title point of view the burden of proof of validity of the diseño was up to the land owner. If, she explained, the land grant was verified by a survey, rudimentary as surveys were in those days, and registered with the new American authorities, ownership was probably valid.

"Was it? I mean in this case?"

"So far, there's no record of its registration. That doesn't mean it doesn't exist. My research of passenger ships and their manifestos shows that the Baron traveled back to Bavaria soon thereafter. Bavaria was an independent country in those days. Later a passenger record shows him having returned to Yerba Buena. I mean, in those days it was around the Cape on a sailing ship—an arduous journey for sure."

Roger asked, "What if the Baron didn't register the grant?"

"Don't know, but I do know most of the Mexican Land grants were properly registered and have been confirmed."

"But not all?"

"Not all. If not registered, then there will be a legal free-for-all lifetime of court trials, hearings, and heaven knows what else. I can image a time, an eternity perhaps, of turmoil."

CHAPTER EIGHTEEN:
LOVE IT HERE

Samantha Smith, a social worker from the Region's closest homeless shelter—all 20 beds of it—doing her daily tour trying to help the homeless, approached a makeshift tent which had been pitched at some distance from other like-looking tents and its neighboring hobbled-together shelters. All of the shelters lay within close proximity to the 680 freeway on-ramp. "Hello, in there," hesitatingly, almost frightened, she called out, peering through the opening into the interior darkness. Maybe this time she would get an answer, but instead of a deranged or worse, a wildly-bearded male with latent revenge etched onto his dirty face, the face that did appear displayed a smile. Cordial, Samantha thought with relief, fearful her moment of comfort would be fleeting. She announced in her trained voice, "Hello there, I'm Samantha Smith from the Region's Homeless Brigade."

"Hello yourself out there. I'm Stewart Churchill from the Union of United Homeless World Citizens." The face laughed, then grew serious as it stared at Samantha in a gaze that was beginning to unnerve her even more. She wished she was back in her office shuffling papers, then reminded herself that researching and talking to the homeless was her job, what she had trained for, and why there were so many credentialed letters on her business card, which she now placed in Mr. Churchill's open palm, careful not to touch skin.

"What can I do for you, Ms. Smith?" Stewart asked, his tone wary, with a touch of friendliness. "Smith? What's your real name? Or don't you want any of us to know?"

Silence from Samantha.

"Sorry," Stewart said softly. "That's my homeless humor… wanna drink?" He reached behind him in the tent and produced a half-filled wine bottle—red—and took a swig. Sheepishly, he added, "I do have cups."

"Ah, no, but thank you," Samantha managed. Composing herself, she reached into her bag and, coming up with a notebook and pen, asked, "I'm doing a survey and I want to ask you why you are here. I mean, were you laid off from work, or ah… are you out of money, or… just why are you here in this place, living in this tent?"

"You homeless, Ms. Smith?"

Taken back, she replied, "Well, no, I live with my grandmother not far from here."

"You're homeless then. Welcome to our special Yerba Buena world."

Samantha made some marks on her survey sheet, a confused look on her face. "Well, then you're not out of work?"

"Work? I tried that after my third year at Harvard. Cooped up in a high rise for 10 yours a day, the noises and complexities of business devouring my spirit, no trees, no birds singing, no fragrances of nature. No, I didn't like it. I didn't want to spend the rest of my life there. Besides, there was no wine to drink, and I do like wine, especially this pinot here." He again offered her the bottle. "Good vintage, good nose," he declared.

"How do you manage?" she asked. "I mean, money wise."

"My dad sends me money once a month, to a bank up the street."

"He supports you?"

"Yeah, so long as I stay away from home and his private club and don't embarrass him and his rich establishment buddies. You know, I'm writing."

"What?"

"A manifesto for justice for the homeless. I'm going to post it on every church door, on every office building, on every library, on everyone's back as they walk past my tent." And he disappeared inside his tent, leaving Samantha the task of making appropriate entries on her survey form.

*　　　　*　　　　*

Medical

She went on to see tents of various designs, various colors, and various shapes, each with various degrees of what some would call litter outside, and probably inside—what those within would likely claim as the extent of their earthly possessions. That was the sight Samantha Smith saw the following day as she made the rounds of her daily homeless monitoring assignment for her civic agency.

Approaching the first tent in the line, she called gently, "Hello. Is anyone there."

"He's at work," a voice said.

Samantha saw a head jut out from the next tent. Assuming that was the source of the voice, she said, "What's your name?"

"Puddin."

"Who is it that is at work?"

"We call him 'Polar' because he ices every question."

Samantha briefly introduced herself and handed her card to the hand of color emerging to accept it. She said cheerfully, "Do you ask a lot of questions?"

"Like, when we goin' to see the doctor. I'm sick."

"What is wrong with you?"

Puddin grew hostile. "Everything. You want me make you a list?"

Samantha handed him a pad of paper and a ballpoint. "Yes, please. I'll take it back to my office."

"And get me a doctor?"

Samantha looked at her manual. "There's a clinic four blocks over." She pointed in the direction.

The voice emerged, crutches in hand. She saw that Puddin's left leg had been amputated above the knee. "Are you a veteran?"

"Nam."

"Thank you for your service."

Puddin spat towards her feet.

Samantha tried, "Have you contacted the Veterans Administration?"

"Yeah, I go there once a year if I can get a bus. But usually the driver won't let me on board and drives off. Scared of me. Anyway I don't have the fare." Samantha wasn't authorized to hand out money or food or booze, for sure. So she moved on down the line of tents.

A woman of indeterminate age, in Samantha's opinion, answered her "hello" at the flap of the next tent. "Who are you and what do you want?" the voice asked in a raspy voice, adding, "You got gifts for me?"

Samantha routinely repeated the applicable portion of her mission statement, "We don't judge, nor do we support, fund, or supply food or supplies to the homeless; we try to help or ease the plight of the homeless in any way we can under the limits of our mission statement."

The woman began to laugh uncontrollably, even after she'd disappeared back into her tent.

Samantha continued her trek along the tent row, stopping at each tent or shelter to hand out a printed flyer about a church-sponsored free dinner in two weeks at a religious facility eight city blocks away.

CHAPTER NINETEEN:
THREATS

The next day in her daily duties, Samantha resumed her inventory of homeless in her assigned territory. Three men were playing dominos on a concrete table in a little park next to a church.

"Who's winning?" she asked, a friendly lilt in her voice.

"The General," one of the men said and gestured toward a man wearing an Army fatigue jacket with stars pinned in several rows on his chest and shoulders. Samantha felt as if she should salute but didn't. "He always wins," the third man allowed.

"Rank has its privilege," the General commented with the wisdom of the ages, and then laughed heartily, underscoring his statement. He looked at Samantha closely and asked, "And what's your rank, soldier?"

"I'm a messenger." She handed each man a flyer about the upcoming church dinner for homeless and said, "Here's the latest word."

"And the word shall set you free," the General commented.

"Wanna play?" one of the men asked, looking at Samantha. "We need more words. Because we all want to set free from this here battlefield strewn with the defeated."

"You're not defeated," Samantha replied, offering in an upbeat tone.

"Sister, once you're down this many points in the game of life, your chances of getting the next rebound are pretty dim, because all the players are taller and practiced at their game. We're serving time in the penalty box of life."

The General smiled at her, stood up and howled loudly as if he were telling the cars on the freeway which off-ramp to take, "Okay, you go back to your social services world and thank them for their service and jump as high as you can because life is one continual jump-ball challenge."

Samantha thanked them and continued on her rounds.

*   *   *

Samantha and her fellow social workers at the Region's local homeless support office feared summer. That was the time when the homeless population seemed to balloon. They had to re-double their efforts to try to see that the children had proper shelter during the summer heat.

Samantha was being accompanied on her rounds by a new person, who had graduated from college with a social services degree. Samantha explained, "Parents who may have temporary housing often lose it during the summer because property owners can make more money with tourist vacation rentals, so out go the parents and their kids—out into the streets of the world. The parents may be able to double up with relatives, but often not. That leaves the kids unaccounted for during the day and often at night. Our agency must provide some sort of shelter and a minimum food ration for each child."

"Where can you do that?"

Samantha said, "A couple of schools open the gyms and playgrounds and make space available with cots. Our agency arranges a food delivery once a day from the Region's local non-profit Food Bank. And you and I, for example, are supposed to monitor the schools and report accordingly.

"What about summer school classes for the kids?"

Samantha shook her head. "No, we're not part of the school district."

"Do they?"

"There's no funding from federal or state agencies. Beside, it's summer vacation for the teachers. But we do get volunteers from the local art collective. Someone from their group comes by once a week or more sometimes. The volunteer brings drawing paper, crayons, sometimes tubes of paints, and lets the kids draw, giving them encouragement."

"How does that work out?"

"Good, so my manager says. He once showed me some photos of the children doing their paintings. He called it 'tent art'. Some of them live in tents and draw paintings on the tent canvas."

The recruit smiled. "Well, how about discipline during the day for the kids?"

"Oh, yes, the police come by periodically."

"Drugs?"

Samantha assured her recruit, "We try to monitor the situation and let the police know if there's anything suspicious going on."

"Parents?"

"They work if they can find jobs. Of course they're concerned and do come by and take their kids away sometimes."

"For good?"

"Maybe, although they have no place to put the kids during the summer months."

"But what about medical care for the children?"

"There's a free clinic."

"Where? How accessible is it? And what do they do there? What if there's an outbreak of some communicable disease?"

Samantha was growing impatient with all the questions. Yet she recognized the legitimacy of the queries and wanted to answer her new associate. As they walked toward another colony of makeshift homeless housing, Samantha said, "I wish I could offer you better answers for what are very germane questions."

The new person said, "But you can't?"

Samantha nodded as they approached a woman pushing two grocery carts overflowing with bags of personal possessions. Atop one bag sat a little furry dog. A small sign around its neck proclaimed, "Dogs can be homeless, too."

*   *   *

Music

Samantha and her recruit heard music up ahead. A raucous voice began singing as a banjo was being strummed. It was a song of lament. A song of the oppressed. A song of those bypassed by society. A downer song, a folk story but sung with feeling as if there was, somewhere, hope to buoy one onward to a possibly (but not likely) realized future, promising a situation better than the present.

They walked on, smiling at the musician, then applauding as he finished. Samantha dropped a few coins in his cup, whispering to her recruit, "I'm allowed a small petty cash for supporting them."

"Small?"

Samantha nodded, then said, "I wish it were more, a lot more, millions more, in fact. Left to our devices, you and I might be able to mitigate the homeless problem."

"But how?"

Samantha puzzled, "I don't know. All I have are thoughts, ideas, worries, and then I lie awake at night, thankful I have a bed, a roof over me, and my grandmother to help fix my breakfast and with whom I can talk. She's the benchmark of my life."

"Whom do homeless people look to for guidance in their lives?"

"Sometimes to us. Then there are churches, other agencies, federal programs, state programs. All with staffs of people."

"Do we see any of them out here in the field?"

"Once in a while. They usually stick to their air-conditioned offices and make plans, draw up charts, issue reports to justify their grants, their funding, and remind everyone they don't have enough money to be effective."

There's one major exception, and that is Project Homeless. It is funded by the Region, just as we are, plus several charities. They and their volunteers hold medical clinics several times a year where homeless can come and get medical examinations, some medicines, drugs, advice, even dental care. A few attorneys come to offer *pro bono* legal advice."

"Why doesn't that solve the homeless problem?" Samantha asked.

"It would if it were held every day so that all the homeless could take advantage of it, but as it is the homeless are so scattered, and without transportation, only those nearby can walk to it. And a lot are on crutches, have walkers and canes, and just not able to physically move around like you and me."

The recruit said, "In other words, it's a start but not a finish."

"A start. And it helps some, but given the vast numbers of the homeless and their being so spread out, it remains a start and not even a progression toward a solution. But consider this program that we want to start."

"Tell me about it."

"Many of the homeless are trying to get jobs. Some hope they can get jobs that will pay enough so they can afford some sort of housing and get off the streets. Trouble is, when they apply for a job they have no address, no email, no telephone. How can you get a job without a telephone number?"

"No way."

"Exactly, so the idea is to give the homeless a telephone with a specific number for them that they can then give out to a prospective employer to follow up with, or that they can use to follow-up their application."

"Cool."

"Takes money, though, and we're still trying to get a grant from several nonprofits to fund the program."

"What's the delay?"

"My supervisor says it's the stereotypes that people harbor about the homeless."

"Which are?"

"They're mentally disturbed and can't qualify for a job anywhere with any organization. They're medically dangerous, have diseases, are unclean and unable to react positively in any sort of social environment, let alone a job situation."

"Any of that true?"

"Some, of course, but there are no real studies to quantify answers, no system to break down the homeless into categories, only meager attempts."

"Is it the case, do you think, that their numbers are growing at a faster rate than the agencies can react?"

"And handle? Yes…" Samantha's voice drifted off.

CHAPTER TWENTY:
THE MEETING WITH ANGELIKA

On a rainy winterish night, the three—Roger, Anna, and Jeremy—met, not in Angelika's private office, where the Region's employees might observe the guests and tweet about the rumored subject matter, or in the communal law offices of Jeremy and Anna where tweets could be read and spread to others across the Internet. Instead, they were meeting in Angelika's and husband Peter's professionally decorated home.

Angelika gave them a tour of her art collection, telling about each artist. Dates of the oil and watercolor paintings ranged across several centuries. Peter summarized their work in restoring the dwelling to its 19th century Spanish Colonial grandeur.

With the high fidelity system playing classical music in the background, Angelika asked Anna to talk about her plan. "You assured me in our phone conversation that I would be interested in your solution to the homeless problem here in Yerba Buena. That's a tall order, but an enticing come-on."

Peter said, "I hope it's not some silly specious scheme."

Roger assured Peter and Angelika, "We wouldn't waste your time with a pie-in-the-sky plan."

"Good," Angelika said, waiting, anticipating.

Jeremy suggested he start by outlining his thinking from the very beginning, and they all agreed. So, he held forth for about 20 minutes setting forth his hypothesis on the law being mired in the past, and that to pursue a solution to the current homeless situation in Yerba Buena, new ides and creativity were required.

Roger said, "The three of us are focused on this huge tract of undeveloped land, the ownership of which goes back to the 1848 Mexican Land Grant. It is now owned by the Bavarian Club through a nominee in the Bahamas. That is, the wealthy members of the club's Board of Directors are the ones we must confront."

"What specifically are you proposing for my agency?" Angelika pressed.

Jeremy explained, "To be specific, as Roger's legal council, we are proposing to your Region that he exclusively represent your agency from a real estate brokerage point of view for the purpose of acquiring this large tract of undeveloped land from the Bavarian Club."

He went on, "Should they decline your purchase offer—and the price will not be mentioned—only that you are a government agency and, for the benefit of all the people, you must acquire the land by filing an eminent domain law suit in your agency's meritorious quest to solve the Region's overwhelming homeless problem."

"Go on," Angelika urged in a voice betraying her excitement.

"We anticipate that the Board of the Bavarian Club will have either ignored or else outright declined your offer to purchase the land. Given their rejection, our firm, on your behalf, will file the eminent domain lawsuit."

"What about just compensation to the owners?" Angelika wanted to know. Jeremy replied, "Here's the key punch line: Our proposal of compensation in the taking clause will be that their acquiescence to your eminent domain legal claim will guarantee that their system of government—as represented by their privileged stature in society—which will continue to be theirs to benefit from—and will no longer be threatened by the unknowns of social unrest with its potentially adversarial and disruptive consequences.

"In other words, their cherished social status will continue to prevail and will not be threatened by some sort of social unrest." He paused and slowly said the dread word "revolution" and then went on, "Because your agency, through the hiring of many different private enterprises, will build sufficient housing to satisfy the homeless problem in all of Yerba Buena, thus removing any threat of serious change or, worse, the threat of the people on the streets overthrowing the system of government and the resultant taking—confiscating, that is—their personal private property. Elimination of such menacing threats, together with the reassurance of the continuation of their untarnished social status will constitute their just compensation, as required by the 5th Amendment to the U. S. Constitution."

Peter chuckled. "Clever."

Jeremy continued, "The proposed housing units you will have built will range from tiny houses to multiple family dwellings, each professionally designed. Construction will have met the standards of the building code, as well as zoning regulations."

Angelika poured herself another glass of pinot, chugalugged and exclaimed, "Wow!"

*   *   *

No one said anything for a few moments as they sat in silence, contemplating the seriousness and the depth of meaning of Angelika's "Wow." Yet she voiced it with a concern evident to the others. Her single word ratified the complexity of Anna's and Jeremy's proposal, perhaps even its impossibility on the scale of things possible in the glossary of the current day's probabilities— getting a complicated proposal into the mental outlook of a diverse group of people, not to mention the general population—land owners, media, which was not likely to understand the nuances of eminent domain, let alone the historic back stories associated with Mexican Land Grants.

Yet, at that very moment, they each realized that they were on to the only feasible and practical solution for overcoming the Yerba Buena homeless situation.

From her designer attaché case, Angelika withdrew a list of members of her Agency's board of directors. "One hundred," She said as if she even needed to voice the number, for they each knew the number. In fact, in that moment of communal acknowledgement, they realized, without verbalizing it, the hurdle they faced. Jeremy knifed the silence by asking, "Angelika, do we need a majority, a plurality, or one hundred percent?"

Angelika extracted another folder and visually whipped through it for an answer.

Before Angelika could state her opinion, Jeremy posed another question, "Do we need a referendum of the voters? That would require the question being put on the ballot at the next election."

"No to that," was Angelika's prompt response. "The staff, through the Board, is empowered to act, under the terms of the referendum approved by the people of Yerba Buena in all the cities and counties therein that created my agency and established the

Region's autonomy. Remember, we'll be acting as a benevolent government agency—in other words, we've got the good of all society on our side supporting our action. By our charter, my agency is empowered to act."

Jeremy reminded, "Back to the question then of the percentage of the Board members needed for approval of such an eminent domain lawsuit."

"Looking it up," Angelika said as she continued to devour her files. They waited. Finally she said, "It appears we will need two-thirds of the Board members to consent to an eminent domain case. However, to be prudent, I'll need to run it by our outside legal counsel.

Anna weighed in. "That could be a problem. I know from what my father has said that two of the lawyers in that outside firm of yours are members of the Bavarian Cub."

Angelika replied, "Then the firm will have to defer. That means referring my question to a different legal firm."

Jeremy turned toward Angelika to ask, "What is the tenor of your Board? Do you think they will go along with your proposed eminent domain action?"

Angelika opened a cupboard and pulled out a colorful box decorated with a variety of animals in a medley of colors—a child's toy box, Jeremy assumed. From it, she scooped out handful after handful of jungle animals, ranging from lions to elephants to giraffe to wildebeest to hippos to tigers. On the table she began, while in deep thought, to form them into groups, whispering out loud mainly to herself, but in a voice strong enough they could all hear. These are "yes," these or "maybes," these are probably "nos."

She looked up and explained tenderly to the others, "My father brought me these carved wooden animals from Africa on one of his safaris." She adjusted the big game animal groups, moving some from one arrangement to anther, and then, mumbling words about each, moved some back where they started. "To display his trophies, he built a special building behind our house in a Chicago suburb. I grew up imagining myself hunting big game, tracking them across their native habitat, and then shooting them and mounting them in my own trophy museum. But of course, I didn't do any of that. Instead I got involved in community service while I was in my second year of college.

To himself, Roger counted 100 animals, one for each board member. When she announced she was done, he mentally tabulated the numbers making up each group. Then he asked, "Which group is which?"

"What I call the 'safari' group is the most adventuresome. They'll most likely go along with my staff's recommendations."

"That means your views," stated Anna, receiving in return Angelika's smile and nod. "How many are in that group?"

"Sixty plus, hopefully." Angelika hesitated. "But we'll need more—two-thirds to three-quarters for a go-ahead… that's my guess as of this evening."

"So, we've got to go hunting for more important trophy animals," declared Jeremy.

Angelika reflected, "Yes, we'll make a list of those we must 'target.' But first, we must put together a written proposal to submit to the board, spelling out our moral and legal reasons for proposing the eminent domain suit. That includes legal verification of the chain of title going back to the original Mexican Land Grant."

Peter said, "Angie, somewhere in here you're going to need an appraisal of the value from an accredited appraisal firm. Even if you're not going to pay out money. Should you win the eminent domain suit, the court is going to want to establish a worth for the property. How about it, Jeremy, Anna, and Roger?"

"Back up a notch," Anna said emphatically. "To win we've got to show that the owners—the Bavarian Club's wealthy members—based upon their saving their sacred society, will retain the rest of their property due to our perpetuation of their social system which they are on top. That's what they will gain while the rest of us in society will see housing for the homeless provided, as a required social service."

Peter broke into the conversation, "Did you see the news this afternoon. A group of homeless, led by a Sergeant Brown, an Afghanistan veteran, has raided the Harper's Ferry Magazine—that's the free weekly publication handed out to riders on the many commuter ferryboats that crisscross the bay. They're holding old Mr. Harper hostage, having tied him to the magazine's printing presses. They've made demands on the Region's authorities, saying they're going to use the presses to publish something called, 'The Homeless Manifesto.'"

Anna said, "This'll change minds in the Bavarian Club. They'll be more afraid of the homeless streaming in from the streets and occupying their sacred club, yanking down their velvet drapes and sleeping on them, drinking their wine and booze and… well…you can picture the frightful images that will run through their minds as they contemplate the end of their comfortable world."

CHAPTER TWENTY-ONE:
ROGER AND MILAN RUNWAY MEET

Early one rainy night before the techies at the nearby Silicon Valley companies would swarm into this popular venue to down their happy hour drinks, they met in a seafood restaurant overlooking the bay. Disguised in a fishing boat slicker that concealed her jewelry, hair, and most of herself, except for the unusual hue of her nails, Ms. Marmon said, "I can't be seen as myself meeting with you. You may be naïve about life, but definitely not about real estate matters."

"My confidence is my self." Then, over Chardonnay, Roger disclosed, "I have been working with a legal firm researching—"

"—Only one? I have several."

Not a surprise, he thought, but does she have several people like himself in tow, as well? He wanted to know the answer, and tried, "Any others like me?" He thought his question off key, to say the least, and was embarrassed. He received no answer, only a small smile. He ventured, "I'm finding out about Mexican Land Grants made, back before the treaty of Guadalupe-Hidalgo—"

"—That ended the Mexican War and gave us all this land." With an arm, she gestured from the shining sea they were overlooking to the hills rising behind them, as her jewelry jingled.

Roger smiled and whispered a "yes." He waited. She waited, giving him a chance to admire her plain and simple disguise. It was almost like meeting with a fisherwoman, had there been any, a hundred years or more ago. The only thing lacking on her part was a fishing rod with the latest in power reels, a chair to sit in while trolling a line with hooks and lures, as well as a strap around her cute middle to hold both her and the bolted down chair on board, waiting for that exciting moment when the blue marlin, swordfish, sturgeon, or monstrous sea bass—the catch—went for the tease of her line.

"So, why are you telling me about some legal firm? Is this newsy bit relevant to your reporting to me?"

Roger quickly replied. "It's part of my duty to you, as well as my hope of getting a listing on this property. Plus, well, we both know the lure of money." He added, "So, we met with her... with Angelika."

"Good." Ms. Vogue sipped her wine. "What's their plan?"

"They're a government agency."

"Of course they are."

"Well, the idea is for them to file an eminent domain lawsuit."

"I thought as much." She downed half of her glass of Napa Valley Chardonnay and rolled her sensuous tongue along her subtly colorful lips. "Now let's talk about my strategy, which you have been hired to follow."

He wanted to retort, "Hey, wait just a damn minute, I'm..." but he didn't, his curiosity about her scheme smothering his indignation at her rudeness.

"You see, Mr. Idaho, this is good news on your part. Plays right into my plan."

Roger thought maybe he... they... actually she... was getting somewhere. "I'm listening."

She ordered another happy round as the bistro began to fill with young people with their incessant chatter, given their fizzing vitality. Then she dropped what Roger took to be the deal clincher. "You see, the head old man at the Bavarian Club... he's chairman of their board of old men... is... well... having an affair with me."

Roger wasn't surprised, but felt he needed to express something. However, all he could muster was a "wow."

"So, what does your attorney propose to do about the issue of 'just compensation'? Some value has to be established for the court to approve an eminent domain lawsuit."

"I know."

"And your answer?" Sipping, she waited.

Roger said, "The idea is that their compensation consists of benefits to them from the Region solving a pressing social problem that if not properly addressed will lead to revolution, in which case their property will have no value, nor will any of their investments, or their club. It's like 1917 in Russia—that's the fear the lawsuit is intended to ignite in them. Their going along with the compensation idea will save themselves and all of established society from political and social disaster.

She smiled. "Good. That'll scare them. That is, if it's properly presented to him... to them, which I will do over our pillow talk."

"And?"

"That'll put him right in line to list the property with you... with us... to get real money for him and his club. And that's when you will make your entry."

"And say what?"

"That you and your boss—and you won't know anything about his and my relationship—have a dozen or so developers ready to act in designing and building homes for the homeless. That's how you'll solve the homeless problem and put real money in their pockets and not goodwill, which won't buy anything."

Roger downed his wine. "Yikes," he exclaimed. "Think of the commissions!" He began to tally, "One whopper for the land, one for each developer, one for each house sale. I'll be rid of the threat of being homeless and instead looking forward to being rich."

"Exactly," she said. "Tons of money for each of us! That's why I hired you, Mr. Idaho." She stood to leave but then said, "We'll need an appraisal of the property's market value. I know just the accredited firm. The head guy owes me."

CHAPTER TWENTY-TWO:
VALUE

Crammed somewhere in their minds, real estate appraisers, in their low-overhead office, retain a ferocious amount of facts. Between memories and files, they offer a compendium of the up or down movement of real estate values in any community.

Jay Atwood & Associates was such a firm. Housed above an automobile repair shop owned by his brother, over the years Jay's one-man firm had developed a reputation throughout the Region as a professional appraiser who could accurately tell a developer, a home owner, a bank, or a mortgage lender what a particular piece of raw land, a building, or a house was worth in the open and free market place of American Capitalism.

Jay had learned first hand the costs of construction when he worked for his uncle in the house framing business. He had also been buffeted about by union negotiations and labor strikes. He had experienced the delays in construction caused by building inspectors failing to show up, sometimes looking for a bribe, other times both belligerent and jealous in their attitude toward the profit racked up by developers, but unwilling themselves to take on the overwhelming financial risks to try to achieve those elusive profits. Jay had also dealt with the complex conditions of the uniform building code. In short, Jay had come face to face with the ingredients that went into the stew that made up the recipe for value in real estate.

But Jay had never encountered a Mexican Land grant, for by the time he went into the business, those Spanish and Mexican land grants had long since been resolved, usually with the grant being subdivided multiple times into smaller and smaller parcels. If there was any portion remaining, it was in the days of Mexican rule when transfers were usually deeded down through the female inheritance line. By today, so Jay had always felt, the grant itself had become irrelevant, for all practical purpose of establishing values on its subdivided parts.

Such was the case until the most powerful real estate broker in the Region climbed the stairs behind his brother's garage repair shop and knocked loudly on his door. Somehow, she had known that on this day and at this hour he was in his office doing research into online records. Usually he was "in the field."

Actually it was not the knock that caused him to look up from behind his 27" desktop computer but rather the jingle of jewelry on her wrists that diverted his attention. "Jay," she called out in her commanding female voice. "Jay Atwood, I have a major challenge for you."

Jay unlocked his door, saw her standing there, as he had expected to, gaped at her for a brief moment of gender appreciation, and then, recovering, invited her in. She plopped herself atop a stack of binders holding parcel maps, crossed her well-appraised legs and smiled at him as if she were a messenger from the angel Gabriel carrying hints of a golden parcel somewhere if Jay would simply pay attention to her message.

"Yes," he managed, finally composing himself enough to suggest she might like a green tea.

"Lovely," she purred.

He found a clean ceramic cup, a fresh tea bag, and poured from his always-hot kettle.

She sipped the brew gingerly and asked with intrigue in her voice, "Have you ever appraised a Mexican Land Grant?"

Jay sensed something special beyond her query question, but replied with only a simple "no." He thought for a moment and added, "No need. They're all parceled out by now."

"What do you think of virgins?"

"A natural human condition."

"How about a virgin land grant?" Her legs moved in sync with her voice.

"Not natural in this day and age." Not as natural as her legs, he commented to himself. Interested in both subjects, he asked, "Where is this leading?"

"To an appraisal," she assured.

"Are you hiring my services?"

"If you have an innovative approach to a virgin situation."

"We appraisers are not noted for innovation, but instead for accurate reporting of values."

"Are you interested?"

Of course, he thought to himself as he replied with a "yes."

She hopped down, moved to stand beside him and extracted a folded map of Yerba Buena from her petite purse. She unfolded the cartography and pointed.

That's the Bavarian Club's huge holding," he stated after visually perusing the property map.

She purred once more and wiggled, their bodies touching. Stick to business, he instructed himself. "And you're saying to me that this parcel remains as the original Mexican Land Grant?"

"Going back to 1848."

"But the club owns it now. Isn't that so? I'd have to look at the chain of title. Surely they are in title."

"Is anything really sure in real estate?"

"But this huge parcel couldn't be just sitting there, given the demand for development in Yerba Buena."

"Unless any prospective buyer would be up against a seller as reluctant as those old men in the Bavarian Club."

"And maybe a clouded title, isn't that what you are hinting at?"

She smiled sweetly. "I do believe you get my drift, Mr. Jay Atwood."

CHAPTER TWENTY-THREE:
A FACTORY FOR HOMES

Angelika, along with several members of her staff, visited the owner of a factory that years before had manufactured homes on what was compared in those days to an automobile assembly line. The factory had turned out a house every day, loaded it onto a trailer, trucked to a home building site somewhere in Yerba Buena. There, it would have been connected to the municipal water supply, the city's sanitary sewer, and an electric utility, and then promptly sold to eager homebuyers. The factory had even arranged for, when asked, long term mortgage financing through an eastern life insurance company. A nice package, Angelika remarked to Ned Dawson, the bearded older factory owner.

"Pardon me," he said apologetically, "while I mop down the cobwebs in my office. You see, we've been shut down for several years, there being virtually no homes being built anywhere in Yerba Buena. No land, you see. Oh, there's the occasional high rise jutting up multiple stories above a rapid transit parking lot somewhere."

"High rises are not your cup of tea," Angelika stated to Dawson's nod.

"Right, all we know how to do is crank out single family homes. Oh, we've done a few stacked unit apartments and condominiums, but even that market is dead today."

Dawson surveyed the assortment of younger people sitting on the dusty chairs in his dusty office and, a puzzled look on his face, asked, "So, what brings you enthusiastic guys to see me today?"

Her staff looked to Angelika to speak on behalf of the agency, which she did, "Well, sir, our agency is looking to sponsor a home building project in Yerba Buena that will require a large quantity of housing. What capacity of housing could you, once you geared up, produce per day or per week? We're thinking of conventional houses, usual size, plus a line of what the media has come to label as 'tiny houses'."

Dawson thought for a moment before replying, "I'd need time to recall my workers, many of whom have gone into re-training programs through local community colleges to learn new trades. Others have found work in the burgeoning remodeling craze. I might be able to hire immigrants, however, who have carpentry and plumbing backgrounds, even if in another country." He thought for another moment and then raised a finger, asking, "What about infrastructure? I mean, utilities, roads, the lifeline connections these houses of yours will have to have in place in order to be livable."

Angelika replied, "Good question. We're planning for a large municipal bond issue that will pay for the installation of those services. We're talking millions of dollars, although we don't have a budget as yet. But we are a taxing authority by virtue of our charter," she explained to Dawson's knowing nod.

"What happens next?" Dawson asked.

"We're interviewing several housing manufacturers—"

—Dawson interrupted, "I'm the only one left in all of Yerba Buena, as far as I know. Every other home builder has gone out of business, as I did, but I still keep my facility here, as you can see, in the hope that someday—"

"—No one else?" Angelika said incredulously.

"No one," he confirmed.

"But there are tradespeople available?" Angelika asked.

"Oh yes, the plumbers, electricians, carpenters—but most of them are hard at work doing remodels for folks who own houses. There's lots of work along those lines. You bet!"

"So, you have a pool of workers to draw upon?"

"A pool, yes, but only in theory, but not necessarily available."

"Why?"

"Well, a project the size you're talking about would have to be a union project. If not, the unions will picket, and for political reasons, the voters will side with the unions. Suppliers will side with them, as well, and the project will be shut down, stymied, deadlocked, blocked. One such as yourself must be political and realistic in a community the size of Yerba Buena. Most of the tradespeople doing remodeling jobs are not union members. Their jobs are too small to warrant union organizing efforts. But once you announce the magnitude of your project, the unions will haunt you day and night for you to become a union shop, where all the contractors involved can hire only union members."

*   *   *

For Angelika's follow-up staff meeting, her top members prepared a list of hurdles to overcome if they were to propose to the Agency's 100-member board of directors the eminent domain lawsuit to acquire the Bavarian Club's huge parcel of undeveloped land in Yerba Buena.

One of the staffers, having prepared the printed handout, thought of another hurdle that so far had not been explored, title insurance. She said to Angelika, "It's my recommendation that we explore this topic with the largest title insurance company in Yerba Buena. So, I have set up an appointment with their president for tomorrow."

*   *   *

Angelika introduced herself and several accompanying staff members to the title insurance company's president, Dominick Wordsworth.

"You want us to insure the title to a Mexican Land Grant?" He asked, surprise and concern competing for dominance in his voice.

Angelika asked, "Yes, but why is that such a daunting request?"

"First off, we've never done that before, and I don't know of any title insurance company that has ever insured a Mexican Land Grant. In this case, according to what your staff person has told me, there's been no change of ownership, apart from setting up a dummy corporation to pay property taxes, since Santa Anna granted the diseño to this Baron Herzog some—how many years ago was it?"

"So, what is the problem?" Angelika wanted to know.

"You see, we've got to essentially underwrite the Treaty of Guadalupe-Hidalgo. And if we're wrong, as determined by some lawsuit, and we have to pay for the title, well, then, we're out of business with a huge loss. And you, or whoever it is that is determined to be the owner, while perhaps wining a lawsuit, is receiving no monetary award because the insurer—that's us—or whichever title company you choose, is out of business because of such a huge claim. I mean, what is the worth of that huge undeveloped parcel in today's crazy marketplace? At least trillions of dollars—how many I can't begin to guess—that is, if you appraise the land at its basic worth, divided as it might be into an unlimited number of 6000 square foot residential lots, or however you might construe its parcelization. So, while title insurance is our business, we're not obliged to accept every premium offered to us any more than any insurance company is so obliged."

And that was that when it came to the subject of title insurance should Angelika's agency prevail in an eminent domain lawsuit. At least, with this particular title insurance company.

CHAPTER TWENTY-FOUR:
THE BIG 100 AND
THE EMINENT DOMAIN LAWSUIT

Angelika and her staff went to work feverishly composing a draft of the official letter they would send by courier to each of the 100 members of the Region's Agency Board of Directors. Most letters would be delivered to their offices, a selected few to their homes. Their efforts to compose the draft took a concentration of staff time, along with the intently focused viewpoint and guidance of Angelika as she parsed the delicate politics of their literary communication.

In the introductory section of the multi-page letter, the staff reported in depth the scope of the homeless problem in Yerba Buena. They cited statistics, as best they had been assembled by independent research organizations nationwide and in Yerba Buena. In heartfelt and emotional terms, they described individual cases of the human impact of living on the streets. They related the magnitude of the sanitary problems being encountered in every part of the vast Yerba Buena Region. In human interest recapitulations, citing specific cases, they told of the dire effects homelessness was having upon families. They told explicit stories of children suffering from either lack of schooling or disruption of their educational programs. They forecast the negative social and political impact on the country of a generation of children reaching maturity with minimal education. They cited the negative effects of lack of proper medical care on those living on the streets. While clinics were available from time to time, they tended to treat emergencies, while not providing ongoing preventative care and holistic health that more fortunate members of the population would receive in their normal doctor-patient relationships, or from their selected spiritual advisors. They told of the emptiness of a life without parental love in the many cases of separated families and of the children in such unfortunate situations being on their own, homeless, left to fend for themselves, day and night, in the streets of Yerba Buena. And finally, remembering those board members who were animal lovers, they reminded the board that dogs and cats also can find themselves homeless.

In the next headlined section, under the title of "The Solution," they literally built their case for preparing and filing the eminent domain lawsuit, which if approved by the court, would allow them to acquire the Bavarian Club's vast undeveloped land holding. For background, they traced the property back to the original Mexican Land Grant of 1848, citing the record of its sale to Baron Herzog and his then entrusting it to the Bavarian Club, which he founded during the California gold rush of 1849.

Then, when and if the property was developed with housing, they argued in their letter to the Board, the entire community—including the current landowners—would benefit through creating the solution to the Region's most pressing social and political problem. Everyone will benefit, they concluded.

As was prudent in seeking support from folks with any new idea, Angelika decided to launch into the tedious task of phoning each of the board members, advising them of the letter they would be receiving in a day or so and of the gravity of the situation. In so doing, she realized, she would be compelled by some members to explain the entire message of the letter, by others she'd expect an "okay, I'll give it my immediate attention," and still others would offer less committed responses.

She attempted to reach each member by cell or by landline. After several days of effort, she had talked to 85 board members, the residual 15 being away on cruises in various parts of the world. She concluded it wouldn't be wise for her to bother them on their tours. To that lot she sent the letter to their home addresses via registered mail, return receipt requested.

*   *   *

Annoying Connections

Angelika philosophized to her staff at their next Monday morning meeting, "Trouble is in communities in America such as ours, those men and women who can be described as 'in charge of society' are not chosen by some higher authority in a contest that rewards those according to their talents and abilities." She added, "These are the people who know people and who vouch for people they know and who, most times, are in debt to return favors to one another."

As she sensed her staff growing discouraged, Angelika said, "Let me quote a sociology professor at a leading university, as follows, 'Organizations are run by and for the benefit of those who are running them.' The goal of most people, then, is to be in the in-group. Our Region of Yerba Buena is no exception," Angelika concluded. To herself, Angelika began to realize there were no exceptions anywhere to the axiomatic rules of society. She reminded herself, "They'll be talking to each other."

After the letters had been distributed, and return receipts had come flooding into the office, it was clear that the issue was on the table, either for further action, board approval, board denial, or maybe worse, board confusion.

"And, do you believe it?" she asked everyone and no one in particular. "Some of our Board members are members of the Bavarian Club."

One staff member asked, "What do we do now?"

Angelika replied, "We wait for the reaction of the board members. Then we'll see if we have a majority backing our eminent domain lawsuit."

*   *   *

Later that evening, Angelika and husband Peter, with their glasses of pinot noir, had come together on their patio, which was stylishly decorated with their collection of Native American Hopi masks and Acoma pottery. In the quiet that comes after each day of duties and dilemmas, Angelika began to talk about her concerns as to the reaction to her letter to her board members. She expressed concerns about the Region's social and political circles in which the board members circulated, and in which they prospered socially.

Peter said, "In the circles inhabited by the technology people and by the investors with whom I have contacts in my company as its CEO, which is separate from your role in political issues, you and I each face similar challenges."

"Define them for me."

"The small number of people who control things, whether it is money or votes, more or less know each other. That is, they went to the same schools, or different schools that played sports with those other schools. That familiarity of education has created a common bond among them. For the most part, they have the same or quite similar tastes, whether it is spiritual affiliations, or car styles—they know their fellow important people who populate the top ranks of society and business. They go to the same vacation places, some to the more luxurious, others to less expensive—but each go to the places that are 'in.' Now, My Dear, you come along with this letter of yours. I have read it. It is well written, well prepared, logical, and states its case professionally. No problems there, as I see it."

"And?"

"Well, Angelika, you've stirred up a hornet's nest of ideas and thoughts, along with the accompanying dilemmas for these prominent folks."

"How so?"

He sipped his pinot and said, "These men and women of power share a broad set of values. Their values are not all the same, for sure, but they are tuned into the same or similar microchips, so to speak. From these sources, they are wired into their own similar guidelines of life. However, in your letter, you have now told them the mental currents that are running in their minds must change from, say, a.c. to d.c."

"'Alternating current' to 'direct current'?"

"Yes, sort of." He smiled. "You're telling them they're going to have to wake up to a system of society with which they are not familiar. And maybe, so you hope, adopt it as their own set of values."

"Which is?"

Peter poured their second glass of wine. "You're telling them that, contrary to their long-held beliefs in American individualism and the rugged and selfish gospel of Ayn Rand, our American society has instead been created for the benefit of all the people—that is, everyone who is alive—not just for the very select prominent few, of which they constitute the elite core."

Angelika stared at her husband. "How else could the letter be written?"

"The letter is more or less perfect as is. It is the fundamental issue you're asking, really telling your board members that they must address. That is what will make them, well, I presume, no, I'm sure, really squirm."

"So, what do you think will constitute their replies to my query letter?"

He asked, "What do think is the answer?" He went on, "Angie, you've crossed the Rubicon. Or, really proposed that you and all of your board and, more far reaching, all of society, must now cross the Rubicon, whether they want to or not, whether they're ready or not."

"It's that serious?"

"In my opinion it is. It's as if I were to tell my investors that the return on their money, on their investment in my company, is not going to pay out in dividends and capital gains, but rather in the concept of happiness for our customers and our workers, and not for the benefit of their pocketbooks. I fear they'd fire me on the spot."

Angelika was stunned. She tried, "But what about the homeless? You haven't mentioned them. Aren't they to benefit somehow from this eminent domain lawsuit?"

"Oh, of course. It's them versus the rest of us."

"Meant to be?"

He smiled and said, "The people who own property, that is, a lot of property, have a lot of money and nurture it. They are quite likely to become philosophically frightened at any hint of change. I mean, frightened if they don't authorize your lawsuit and frightened if they do, because of the sea change to their lives such an eminent domain threatens to bring. It's a whopper of an unknown for them, and moneyed interests eschew unknowns."

"So what will be the outcome?"

"I'm scheduled for an investor meeting in the morning… early. They'll probably have heard about the letter. I'll let you know if there's any feedback offered among my investors on the subject of eminent domain."

CHAPTER TWENTY-FIVE:
"GOODY'S" PILLOW

She allowed the monogrammed sheet to fall away from one of her shoulders in a seductive maneuver that positioned her to look lovingly into "Goody's" unshaven face. "My Precious Dear," she purred, "it's your decision. Your board will follow you. They always do because they believe, as I do, that you have the wisdom, the experience in important matters of this sort."

Eyes on her, all of her, he nodded.

"So allow me to advise you."

"I usually do."

She smiled as the sheet fell farther down.

In his delight, he queried, "Yes?"

"This lawsuit—"

"—Lawsuit?"

"Yes, the eminent domain lawsuit that, if approved, promises to take away your club's land."

"That's the one being filed by my daughter and her homeless husband…"

"Yes. She and he are homeless."

"Goody" bristled.

"Just sayin' what's what."

"I told her I'd help, but his FICO score is so low they can't qualify for a free cup of coffee at one of those shelters."

"Set that aside for the moment, My Man."

He did and slowly and approvingly, of course, appraised her terrain. "So, My Lovely, what is this advice of yours you are about to give me?"

"I'm telling you that you will look much better with your board and all your club members of your great club if you avoid this lawsuit."

"Why is that?"

"Because, My Handsome, you may lose, given the mood of the courts today. And if you do lose, your club will receive no compensation, and you and your friends will have to part with your huge piece of undeveloped land received from Baron Herzog all those years ago. There will be no more first growth redwoods for you and your buddies to admire, no more high jinks for you men to have fun with while roughing it in your little tents. All will be past history. Your financial losses—and they'll be big—will be dedicated to save society."

"Fuck the homeless. Fuck society!"

"Exactly. Better, instead, you and your club receive a lot of money, don't you think, don't you want?"

"Yes, of course. I... the club members... always need more money."

She smiled. She leaned closer, her jewelry playing the tune of allure. "Money always helps. Especially when it comes time to give to your favorite charities that you and your fellow members work so hard for. And to get your precious income tax deductions."

"Goody thought and then, smiling, asked, "What are you trying to tell me, My Sweet?"

She put her bare hand on his arm and told him, "A friend of mine will sell your property, almost overnight, to a number of developers. You can close escrow right away. It'll mean real money in your club account, a huge lot of money. And there'll be no eminent domain lawsuit hanging over you day after day. Dogging you. Incessantly. Consuming your life, your every waking moment, and that of your fellow board members, as well."

"How much? Can we get, I mean?"

"My appraiser is finishing his appraisal." She changed the subject, "You'll like my guy Roger. He's much like you. Lots of ideas, Strong, Capable."

He watched her starting to dress. "When."

"Now. Lunch. In one of your club's private dining rooms. Name's Roger. He's from Idaho."

"Goody" smiled at her. "My father's from Idaho. Made a fortune in potatoes, you know?"

"I do know."

CHAPTER TWENTY-SIX:
THE JUDGE

As Superior Court Judge Michael McKittrick parked his electric sedan by the charging post outside his garage and plugged the charger cord into the receptacle under the front hood, he took scant notice that his wife's color-matching electric SUV was being charged next to his at the other of their matching posts.

Clutching his leather case, the Judge let himself into the house through the carved double-entry doors, entered the Carrara marble-tiled veranda and crossed the foyer. Greeting him were his pair of tail-wagging greyhounds, both of whom he perfunctorily petted.

Judge McKittrick managed a good evening to Luis, his male house servant, nodded that he would like his scotch, entered his bookcase-lined study, briefly admiring his Me-Wall of black and white and color photographs of himself shaking hands with prominent men and women, including celebrities, corporate presidents, and state and federal elected officials. He bid a cursory salute to his favorite now-antique photo of himself kicking the winning goal in his college's playoff soccer match.

Facing him from across his desk as he sat in his ergonomic leather chair was a later casting of a Remington bronze sculpture, "Coming Through the Rye." As usual, the charging horses inspired him to match their vigor, along with that of their mounted cowboys, as he opened his case and began to address his court's upcoming docket.

Luis arrived with an engraved glass of scotch neat and a plate of cheese and crackers, lest his judicial mind's brilliance be ever-so dulled by even that first sip of alcohol, of which he immediately partook.

"Eminent domain," he spoke the words out loud. "Luis," he posed, "do you have the right to take my property from me?"

"Well, no sir, of course not."

"Nor I from you."

Luis puzzled. "But what if the court says it's okay?"

"If I am justly compensated."

Luis nodded. "Yes, compensated." He thought for a moment. "But who is to decide the fairness of the compensation?"

"A judge like me, Luis. I will decide."

"You are a fair judge, Sir."

"So my classmates and my friends at the Bavarian Club tell me." The judge smiled with pride as Luis bowed slightly and turned to leave.

CHAPTER TWENTY-SEVEN:
SEAN O'FLANNERY'S HEIR?

Anna and Jeremy continued to delve into the story of Mexican Land Grants. They discovered that all land grants, to be valid and accepted under California law, had to have been translated into English from the original Spanish. In the California State Archives, that had survived the 1906 Earthquake, then removed to Glendale, and then soon to the National Archives in Washington, DC, they found Sean O'Flannery's Mexican Land Grant. It had been translated into German.

"What do we do now?" Jeremy asked, Anna having shared with him this new information.

"The transfer to Baron Herzog may be invalid."

"Then title would revert back to Sean O'Flannery?"

"Yes."

Roger was told of this development. "Then we've got to translate it into English and make a new claim. Right?"

Anna thought. She looked at Jeremy. Together, they nodded.

Roger asked, "Does Sean have heirs?"

Anna said, "Galway, here we come."

CHAPTER TWENTY-EIGHT:
THE ROUNDUP

All around the Region of Yerba Buena, in the dark of the chill night, homeless persons embraced blankets, sleeping bags, huddled in their tents, oblivious to the never-ending din of traffic noises from the buses, cars, trucks, and jet planes roaring overhead as they approached their landing, or rose higher as they lofted from one of the Region's three major airports. All this while the screeching commuter trains died at their scheduled midnight terminations.

Quiet tried to take over Yerba Buena. A gallant effort at civility. Yet civility was far from the minds of those in their tents, those in blankets lying on the cold hard concrete, those crowding the shelters set up by persons with compassion and money, outnumbered in their charities as they were by the hordes of their adopted charges.

As the night wore on, had a reporter, or a platoon of reporters, been able to capture the thoughts of the homeless, were they to be expressed, from one tent to the next, from one blanket to the next, from under one freeway off-ramp to the next signposted on-ramp, the story might have been the same, but no, the story was to be as varied as the people the reporters hoped would be telling their personal stories. Indeed, there were not enough reporters, and too many homeless persons for each and every story to be told, to be recorded, to be reported to those who might care to read a special edition of the digital or printed press.

Nearby, in the comfort of their single family homes, their condominiums, their co-ops, the people with sufficient income, sufficient assets, the highest of FICO scores, were either sleeping off the parties attended the night before in the clubs and venues like the Bavarian Club or, since Sunday was beginning to dawn, were preparing for church. Priests were polishing their homilies, pastors their sermons, rabies their messages. Be good. Do unto others as you would have them do unto you. That's the word. And the word shall set you free. Be assured of that. Be assured of...

Meanwhile the Yerba Buena Health agency trucks, manned by space-suited workers were cruising the streets, calling out on their microphones for those who didn't make it through the night. Softly they ordered, "Throw Out Your Dead."

To one such command, one homeless opened the flap of his tent and called back, "Throw out your American Dream."

–The End–

END NOTE
JOIN A LEGACY CLUB, IF YOU QUALIFY

You can declare your presumably patriotic legacy to the United States of America and Western Culture by joining one or more of any number of legacy clubs. That is, if you are able to prove, that is, document your lineage back to a founding member or founding celebrity. Usually that means either to the American Revolution or a not-so-distant-in-time war or historical event.

For example, if your ancestors fought in the American Revolution and you're a male, and you can prove your lineage back to the fighter, you are eligible to join the Sons of the American Revolution. If you are female, given the same strict procedural rules, you may qualify to join the Daughters of the American Revolution.

These organizations hold annual conventions, reenact Yankee Doodle, publish literature, and together, celebrate their claim upon the story of American history. For the DAR, this includes the original preservation of Washington's home at Mount Vernon on the shore of the Potomac River.

If one of your ancestors came over on the Mayflower, there is the Mayflower Society with its similarly sacred obligation to preserve and honor those early brave colonists and their struggle to face and conquer a hostile but fertile new continent.

If an ancestor fought in the War of 1812-14 against the British, there is a similar type organization for you to join.

The Civil War, aka The War Between the States, presents more opportunities for membership, including, with proof of lineage, joining the Sons of the Confederacy.

If you are descended from an officer in the Continental Army or the French Army fighting with the American Colonists against King George III, you may be eligible to join the Society of Cincinnatus, founded by George Washington and the Marquis d Lafayette to memorialize the military leadership of the American Revolution.

Each of these organizations has a staff of people to administer their activities, a headquarters and a library of books and writings commemorating their existence.

The list of legacy organizations is long. This list is not meant to be complete.

To the list can be added the Los Patricios, the American rebels from Ireland who fought for Mexico in 1846, '47, and '48. Their organization is alive and active in Clifden Town, Galway, honoring their legacy. It continues to be noted by the Irish Literary and Historical Society in San Francisco and, as well, in Phoenix by the Irish Heritage Museum. The music and lyrics from the Irish ballads of the San Patricios continue to be played and sung with feeling and vigor by singers across Ireland, and can be seen and heard on You Tube.

OTHER WORKS BY JON FOYT

Previous Fiction by Jon Foyt (writing with Lois Foyt)

Last Train from Mendrisio
A tycoon sets up an offshore trust

Postage Due
Mother Dear becomes Queen of Albania

Marathon, My Marathon
Nuclear Waste disturbs a cross-border marathon

The Portrait of Time
Native American spirituality competes with an evangelist

The Architecture of Time
Preservation versus a bullet train's right-of-way

Out of Print

The Landscape of Time
The 1808 untold story of the Erie Canal's origin

The Test of Time
A Cleveland socialite joins the WACs in WWII

Screenplays

Painted Waters
a Zuni Pueblo portrait artist meets a
cyberspace evangelist and an Irish journalist

A Nuclear Tide
Nuclear waste storage

Marathon, My Marathon
Adapted from the novel

Time to Retire
Adapted from the novel

Current Fiction by Jon Foyt

The Gilded Chateau
The fifth suit is Gold, as bridge was played in a Swiss Chateau
by central bankers of the WWII warring nations

The Mind of an American Revolutionary
Founding Father Robert Morris

Time to Retire
Mystery and romance in a retirement community

Marcel Proust in Taos
A Los Alamos physicist retires to Taos and finds romance

The Sculpture of Time
Shakespeare's "The Winters Tale" set in California

ABOUT THE AUTHOR

photo by Helen Munch, Victoria, BC, 2013

A native of Indiana, Jon Foyt began writing novels and screenplays with his late wife, Lois Foyt, in 1992. A distance runner, he has finished 60 marathons. He holds degrees from Stanford in Journalism and Geography plus an MBA. He also has completed class work for an Historic Preservation masters at the University of Georgia.

Foyt's other careers have included radio broadcasting, banking, and real estate development in Oregon and California. Jon is an active participant in the retirement community of Rossmoor in Walnut Creek, California. He has three children, eight grandchildren, and two great-grandsons.

AUTHOR'S CREDO

Jon Foyt does little to promote his work because: A) He doesn't like to self-promote, and B) it takes time away from conceiving, researching, and writing the next novel and the next novel after that.

Instead of allocating time to social network, racing after bookstore signings, and pleading with book reviewers, Jon, at age 85, says he wants to write about characters who explore topics and situations he feels have been overlooked.

He does hope people will read his novels. Comments can be emailed to him at jonfoyt@mac.com. He will gladly reply. Jon's website: www.jonfoyt.com

BIBLIOGRAPHY
Homeward Bound

The following sources were consulted for this novel:

Pryor, Alton, *The Mexican Land Grants of California,* Stagecoach Publishing, Roseville, California, 2017

Miceli, Thomas J., *The Economic Theory of Eminent Domain Private Property, Public Use,* Cambridge University Press, 2011

Robinson, William Wilcox, *Land in California, The Story of Mission Land, Ranches, Squatters, Mining Claims, Railroad Grants, Land Scrip, Homesteads,* Hardpress Publishing, Miami, FL, reprint from the University of California Press, 1948

Bohakel, Charles A., "Litigation over state land grants in 1800s proved difficult." *East Bay Times,* April 23, 2008

Made in the USA
Columbia, SC
26 September 2018